A Cameo For a Cowgirl

Carolyn Miller

ONE

Three Creek Ranch might be only thirty minutes from the hustle and bustle of Calgary's high-rises, but it may as well be a million miles away. A different world away. A century—more —away. Cassie James leaned back in the saddle, stroking Ginger's mane as she took in the view, her heart swelling with contentment. From her position on this rise, the ranch's hills and valleys soared and dipped as they stretched toward the higher peaks of the Canadian Rockies, with not a sign of human habitation anywhere to be seen. Instead, she gazed upon trees and grassy meadows, the occasional deer or bird, and the three creeks that gave the ranch its name. The scenery was as it had been for hundreds of years, and for the past century or so that Cassie's family had lived here.

She gently nudged Ginger and the palomino turned obediently in a half circle, bringing into view the ranch's small western town. The buildings—everything from a steepled white chapel to a wooden boardwalk-lined collection of stores—had formed part of an original settlement, once upon a time. But the village had lain empty for years, superfluous as larger centers thrived. Then after the depression hit, forcing the last of the inhabitants to sell, Cassie's great grandfather had expanded the family acres, swallowing the town in its entirety. Not all of the town was original—the schoolhouse and Silver Spur saloon had been trucked in from a hamlet an hour away—but the township was so complete, a perfect representation of pioneer life, that it had been used as a movie set for nearly twenty years.

She might've been a little girl when her parents had first mentioned the possibility of a movie company coming to film on their ranch, but she remembered it like yesterday.

Her dad had been so excited. "The producers love it here, love the fact it looks so unspoiled, with no modern-day trappings. And they're willing to pay us to use the town," he'd said. "Our ranch has to diversify. We can't survive on just cows these days."

Of course, it had helped that the Hollywood company had decided after filming that it was easier to offload the props, sets and costumes, selling them at a fraction of their cost to her folks rather than pay to transport them elsewhere. That had led her parents to the momentous decision to expand Three Creek's operations into including a western movie set and backlot business as well, something that had fascinated Cassie for years, and something she'd taken responsibility for since graduating college five years ago.

So, while she still helped her dad around the ranch as much as she could, she had near total charge of ensuring the day-to-day running of the western town went smoothly. This meant everything from repairing buildings, and checking the prop and costume barn was watertight and pest-free, to fielding enquiries and taking bookings, to being the point person while a production company was in residence.

And today would see the return of the crew of the company filming *As The Heart Draws*, the historical TV show that had taken millions of viewers around the world by storm. People, like her, who longed for a simpler life, a good life. A time when good was good and evil wasn't marketed as normal, or fun, or exciting. Over the years the ranch had played host to a number of famous actors, including Lincoln Cash, whose Hollywood career had skyrocketed since his appearance on the show several years ago.

Lincoln had been easygoing, even willing to sleep on-site in the accommodations Cassie had helped her dad create in some of the buildings. The show's heroine, Ainsley Beckett, was another unpretentious type, perhaps because she'd been with the show since the beginning. Her blossoming career meant she was involved in other things as well now, but any day she was on set was a good one. Ainsley was super sweet, just like the character she played on *As The Heart Draws*. Viewers loved Abigail, the school teacher played by Ainsley, and her Canadian Mountie love interest.

But Cassie had heard that Abigail's brand-new husband had been killed off—thanks to a conflicting Marvel movie schedule—which meant this season would see a new man in the school-teacher's life. Not that viewers knew this yet, as that season's cliffhanger hadn't yet aired. Cassie's site manager role meant she was privy to all kinds of insider gossip, which had seen her sign a non-disclosure contract as well, ensuring her mouth stayed shut. Not even her parents knew that Abigail was getting a new beau, along with a scenario ensuring viewers would be in for another few seasons of "will they? won't they?" as they negotiated the ups and downs of attraction before finally admitting they cared for each other and embarked on a relationship.

Such drama seemed like overkill to her. Why couldn't two adults just have a mature conversation and admit they liked each other instead of teasing it out for so long? Drama for drama's sake was way too complicated for her taste.

It wasn't that she didn't understand hurdles in a relationship. Her brother Franklin had certainly experienced his own challenges with trying to date local sports reporter, Hannah Wade, thanks to Hannah's job. But they'd sorted it out, and were getting married in just a few weeks. Cassie had her own experiences with men who were needy in various ways—most often a need to prove their superiority—but a busy girl didn't have time for playing games. It was just too much fuss. If she ever met a guy she liked, she'd let him know she was interested, without such shenanigans.

But it was precisely such shenanigans that meant the show could go on—and Three Creek Ranch would get paid—and the viewers would stay enthralled, both at the storyline and acting as much as the glorious scenery that brought every episode to life.

She drew in another breath, the crisp morning air holding a reminder of early spring, even as the clear skies promised summer. Oh, she loved it here. Call her conservative—various high school and university boyfriends sure had—but she was proud of her family's legacy that allowed for an untainted landscape, that made it possible for people to escape into this world where the good guys ultimately won, and the bad always got what they justly deserved. Her family's and her own Christian values shaped what movies and TV productions they allowed to be filmed here, which was why the occasional enquiry had to be rejected, as it didn't fit the ranch's "family values."

As a repeat client, *As The Heart Draws* was always welcome, and she knew the sixteen-week schedule they'd booked for would be busy. She'd negotiated for a weekend off at the end of June to allow for her NHL player brother's wedding. Franklin and Hannah—who'd been Cassie's friend since high school—were due to use the chapel and a wedding tent rental for their celebrations, and the logistics of preparing for the huge number of guests were already starting to stress Cassie. Why she'd said yes to helping Hannah when Cassie already had huge responsibilities with the TV show was a mystery. Except it wasn't really. Hannah was her best friend, and Franklin her favorite brother. Her only brother, but whatever. She might have workaholic tendencies—ranch life had taught her and her siblings the value of hard work from a young age—but she'd do anything to help make the day run smoothly and their dream wedding day come true.

She patted Ginger's mane, enjoying the early hour, her favorite time before the day began. The time when peace would steal across her heart and remind her that while she wore a number of hats—movie set manager, ranch hand, cowgirl, daughter, sister, friend—that God was ultimately in control. The wedding would be fine, everything would run smoothly. And the new TV production would go well, and would surely help the ranch's bottom line. "In Jesus's name."

In the distance, a small cloud of dust drew her attention. She squinted then exhaled, recognizing the line of trucks that signaled the arrival of the production company.

"Come on, girl." She nudged Ginger and took the shortcut down the hill in order to help their arrival at the prop barn and office where she'd arranged they would meet.

She arrived at the white barn and dismounted, tied up Ginger, and dusted off her gloves and jeans. Then pushed back her shoulders, her white cowboy hat tipping back as she lifted her chin, smiled, and drew forward to greet Lance Fidler, the show's location manager she'd dealt with before. Yes, today would be a good day. She could feel it.

A sea of expectant faces gazed at him, their smiles almost as big as his as he clutched the golden figurine. Pride filled him as he grinned and lifted the trophy high. "Thank you so much. You'll never know—"

Bleep bleep bleep.

Harrison Woods cracked open a bleary eye as the alarm cut through his dreams. He groaned, then reached out a hand to tap off his phone. Let the day begin.

He rolled out of bed, staggered to the bathroom, then showered. Wrapped a towel around his waist, and smeared the fogged-up glass to study himself in the mirror. Winced. That face sure wouldn't be winning any awards anytime soon. Anytime ever, the way he was going. And now, with this TV show he was still in two minds about, even though Richard Kneever, his agent, kept insisting that playing Special Constable Nathaniel Fraser was an awesome opportunity, he probably could kiss goodbye to any chance of ever being considered a serious actor. *As The Heart Draws* might have millions of fans around the world but come on. Honest talk? It was next door to being a TV soapie. And after just missing out on a gritty part in the latest Nicole Kidman and Reese Witherspoon collaboration, stepping into a Mountie role first made famous by Lincoln Cash was not exactly where he'd envisioned himself this time last year.

A faint memory of an old verse his grandma used to say tried to poke through his mental haze. Something about how a man could plan his course but God would determine his steps. Huh. Weird. Whatever. He yawned, stretched, then snatched up the fallen towel, and hurried to get changed. There weren't any paparazzi cameras here, but a man could never be too careful. And with it being his first day on set at a new job he needed to be extra careful.

He quickly ate his breakfast—the hotel's room service had got his eggs order wrong again—then packed, and walked out to his Camaro. Sure, it looked a little fancy for these parts, but it was warmer now, and with any luck, he might get the chance to take the top off soon.

Thirty minutes later he was following the audio cues of his CarPlay's navigation system, frowning as he drove west along Highway 1. Maybe he should've taken the offer from Maxine, the production assistant assigned to him, and agreed to a driver, after all. He had a feeling he'd missed the turn-off. A sign to Canmore flashed past, triggering another memory. Hadn't the directions said something about the set only being half an hour from the city center? He'd now been driving more than that, surely. He pulled over, hazard lights flashing, and checked his phone map. Hissed out a word. Then waited for a break in the traffic to rejoin.

A peek at the car clock wrinkled his nose. He'd now be pushing it to be on time. Way to go to make a good first impression. Well, second impression for some. He'd obviously made a good enough first impression with the director and producers in order for them to hire him. But for the rest of the crew, if he didn't hurry, he'd show up late like an arrogant you-know-what who expected the world to revolve around him. Which he wasn't. And didn't. Which meant he needed a way to turn around. Pronto. But with no overpass in sight, and only the occasional potholed crossroads to farms or ranches that allowed zero margin of error—and certainly weren't built for low-slung vehicles like this—he'd have to wait a little longer. Great.

He eyed his phone, toying with calling Maxine and giving her an explanation for why he'd be late. But from their previous interactions, he was pretty sure she already didn't think highly of him. Apparently daring to complain about wanting his meals hot and not lukewarm might do that. Who knew? Regardless, he didn't want to add to her load unnecessarily—or add to her low opinion.

Breath exhaled as an overpass appeared in the distance. Thank goodness. He flicked on his signal lights and veered off the service road, then had to wait to rejoin the road circling back to the highway as a huge truck trailer laden with logs inched its way past. He tapped the steering wheel, impatience writhing within. He supposed he could blame the navigation system, although really, it was his own need to make the most of the creature comforts of a hotel room before he was supposed to stay on-site at the ranch where they were filming.

Ugh. When Richard had first mentioned living on-site, Harrison had been tempted to say no. But his agent had assured him there would be a trailer outfitted with all the modern conveniences. Just as well. He didn't do rustic accommodation. Had vowed never to live that way again, after a childhood where his dad drank away the rent money, forcing them to one-bedder dives and trailer parks. And he'd certainly never done camping. He'd have no idea even where to begin. This TV show being filmed mostly outdoors would be enough of a challenge for him. Especially given he'd be expected to ride horses.

Harrison winced. He knew how to ride a horse, but the last time he'd done so had been back in his mid-twenties, over half a decade ago. Fortunately, his audition this time around hadn't depended on his horsemanship skills. He suspected the casting director had seen footage from previous jobs, including from his breakout role on TV, where a random episode had him riding a horse along the beach in a gratuitous shirtless moment. Ugh. At least this show meant he'd be keeping his shirt on. But he wasn't looking forward to revisiting the nitty gritty of horse-riding.

He *was* looking forward to acting opposite Ainsley Beckett. Industry gossip said she was as nice as she was pretty. Last he'd heard, Ainsley wasn't dating anyone, and despite what Marcia—the most recent of his exes—might think, he was flying solo these days. But he'd be willing to reconsider that if he and Ainsley hit it off. Their onscreen chemistry so evident in his audition might well translate to offscreen also. A man could hope, right?

But Ainsley and a decent pay packet were about the only advantages he could see. Despite what Richard said, Harrison still wasn't sure if this was a good career move or just a stop-gap while he waited for his true big break. Historical drama aimed at conservative-leaning women sure wasn't the gritty police detective series Lincoln Cash was now doing. But even Linc had done a stint on this, so who knew what lay in Harrison's future?

His gaze flicked to his phone more than a few times as he carefully navigated to the ranch. He didn't trust the directions pumped out by the onboard system anymore. He swung right, onto a side road, then followed it slowly, as evidence of the past winter was made plain by the road's corrugated ridges and shallow dips. Another glance at the clock and he groaned aloud. It was already ten minutes past the designated arrival time. Definitely not the way to start.

A large sign advertising the Three Creek Ranch, Western Town and Backlot was placed near a gate that led to a long avenue of poplars. He steered his convertible past the gate, the anxiety within easing a little at the glorious view. The Canadian Rockies soared ahead, dressed in spruce and fir, some distant mountains still wearing caps of snow. It might be late spring, almost summer, but he could imagine how cold it would get around here. He'd heard reports of deep minuses in Albertan winters, minus forty or worse. He shuddered. Imagine having to live here in temperatures like that. He was thankful to have a place in LA for most of the year that he could rent out when he wasn't staying there.

His lip curled as a rough wooden frame overhung what looked like the drive to the ranch house. He peered more closely. Yep. A two-storey ranch house with a steep-pitched roof lay at the end of another drive. But that wasn't where he was headed. He followed the arrowed sign to the Western Town and Backlot, passing reddish-brown cattle grazing nearby. He drove over a slight rise, past another forested hill on which perched a rustic-looking farmhouse that had clearly seen better days, that he recognized as one of the sets from his viewing of the show. A sign warning of a "Texas gate" was immediately followed by the teeth-rattling car suspension testing of a cattle guard. Yep, a true ranch. The road led past a large red barn then down to where a spacious parking area was bordered by a clump of trailers and several portable buildings, next to a tree-covered hill. They sure liked their trees around here.

A silver-haired man dressed in a yellow hazard vest held a clipboard—so old school—and gestured for Harrison to slow from his snail-like pace. Harrison powered down the window as he braked.

"Name?" the man barked. His nametag read *Hector*.

He cleared his throat. "Harrison Woods."

"Cast or crew?"

Wow. Good to know he was unrecognizable around here. "Cast." He almost added "Leading man" but figured that wouldn't go down well. But sheesh. Didn't this man know who Ainsley Beckett's new hero was meant to be?

"You're late," Hector said.

"I know that," Harrison gritted out.

"The rest of the cast is doing a walk-through of the town with some crew, so you better hurry."

He bit back a sigh. "Where should I park?"

Hector gestured behind him. "Anywhere'll do."

Anywhere? Didn't this place have designated parking places for leading cast members and crew? He cleared his throat. "Where is the western town?"

The man pointed to the tree-clad hill. Harrison nodded, then drove his Chevy to the nearest available spot and parked. He grabbed his phone, then, after stepping outside, reached in and grabbed his leather jacket as well. It might be almost summer, but that breeze held plenty of chill still. He nodded to another worker, then hurried up the hill.

Another glance at his watch said he was only thirty minutes late. That wasn't too bad. He'd been on some sets where people hadn't shown for several hours. He wasn't that late, at least. And Mal Hendricks, the show's frontrunner—lead writer and director —had been pretty easygoing in their interactions so far. Not that Harrison wanted to push things on day one.

He was sweating by the time he crested the hill—he didn't usually jog in a leather jacket—and forced his breathing to slow as he surveyed the scene. Huh. It really did appear old. From this vantage point, the wooden buildings splayed around the dirt track looked like they'd been here for a century or so. A score of single and two-storey wooden shingled buildings led down to what looked to be old railroad tracks and a white steepled chapel at the end of the dirt street. Whoever cared for the place had done an impressive job. The buildings looked weathertight and well-cared for, apart from a couple that appeared obviously worn, no doubt to provide contrast. A couple of buildings held wooden facades behind which lay white canvas tents, like the true olden days. It must be a huge job to care for this.

He glanced around. Not a modern antennae or powerline to be seen. If he hadn't just seen the backlot and all those cars he could believe himself to be the only one here, transported back in time five generations. He pushed out a reluctant smile. Maybe this wouldn't be so bad, after all. Especially if the catering was okay, and they served hot food and hotter coffee. And nobody hated on him for being a little late on his first day.

A collection of people emerged from the church, and he pushed back his shoulders. He wasn't too sorry to have missed that. The church might only be a set, but he'd be happy to avoid it just the same. He may be an actor, but there was no point pretending he had any use for God these days. God certainly had no use for him.

He hurried past several white-trunked aspens and behind a building, working to avoid being seen. If he could join the little crowd and pretend he'd been here a while, that might be best. He slipped behind a saloon, then realized the door was unlocked, and he could go inside. So he did.

Inside was dim and dark, but even with the small square windows only allowing a little light, he could appreciate his surroundings. The rough timber poles holding up the wooden slatted roof were decked in animal skulls and pelts—an animal lover's hell, as all of them looked real. Oak barrels lined one wall, while another held a few rickety-looking tables and chairs, and a third held a very ancient bar. But even this looked authentic, with uneven shelves displaying a collection of brown and dark glass bottles, along with some earthenware tankards and drinking glasses of various shapes and sizes. Above him hung several oil lanterns, and the huge white skull of what looked like a bighorn sheep. Hmm. If each building was dressed this way, it really could be interesting, and a great way to get in character.

He stroked a pelt—coyote, maybe?—then stilled as a creak came from outside. Uh oh. But he didn't have time to get to the back entrance. He slid behind the front door, hoping that whoever was outside would either not feel the need to come inside, or if they did, the door would swing inwards and hide him. Looking like he was playing hooky in the saloon was definitely not the impression he needed to be making, especially on his first day. He stood in the shadows, waiting.

A murmur of voices came from outside. Then a woman's voice, pitched low.

"And this is what we call Harry's Saloon—"

He froze. What did she say?

"—and another of the original buildings from when it was a town. You'll see it's not nearly as nice inside as the Silver Spur, but it's a good contrast with its skulls and furs, all of which came from here on Three Creek Ranch property."

The door pushed open, and he slunk back further, thankful for its screen. Now to hide behind the door and hope nobody came in. From his position, behind the door yet near a window, he could see people standing outside on what looked like a real wooden boardwalk. He sure hoped they'd all stay outside. It'd be just his luck to have—

Oh, great. Someone entered, moving inside far enough that he could see it was a woman. His nose wrinkled. Her white cowboy hat and leather-fringed jacket marked her as a production assistant who'd gotten a little carried away with the western theme.

She turned on her booted heel, her blue jeans clinging to long legs, one arm gesturing inside as she smiled to those still outside, before pivoting back slightly.

Then her gaze met his, and her smile fell away as she gasped. But before he had a moment to process what was happening, she'd grabbed the door and rammed it into him.

He yelped, rubbing the side of his head as he saw stars. "What the—?"

"What are you doing in here?" she demanded.

Great question. How to explain without looking like even more of a fool than he already appeared?

He knew this was a day he should've stayed in that cozy hotel bed.

Two

"Cassie?" someone asked.

Cassie ignored him, laser-focused on the suspicious guy still hiding in the saloon's shadows. Her fist clenched. She wasn't opposed to violence—hello, her brother played pro hockey in the NHL, and she knew how to use her fists as well as a gun— and this stranger had to be shady. Why else was he still hiding?

"Who are you? What are you doing in here?"

"Cassie?" Mal Hendricks, the director and one of the show's producers, moved inside. Peered behind the door. Then chuckled.

Um, excuse me?

Then the creepy dude seemed to transform before her eyes, straightening, his shoulders broadening as he moved from the shadows, slapped on a grin and held out a hand. "Mal."

"Harrison! Glad you could make it."

Wait. They knew each other?

"Yeah, sorry about that. Blame poor directions."

Cassie stiffened. Hello? Her directions were perfectly fine, thank you very much. Everyone else had managed to get here on time without any problems.

Mal chuckled again. "We wondered if you'd gotten a little lost."

"Lost in a saloon?" she muttered, crossing her arms.

Mal glanced at her. "What was that, Cassie? Oh, I should introduce you to Harrison Woods, our leading man."

His leading man. Definitely not hers. She eyed the hand Harrison offered, taking more than a speck of pleasure as he lowered it, unshaken. "Why exactly were you hiding in here?" she demanded.

Harrison's blue eyes narrowed, his features losing any hint of apology from seconds earlier as he shrugged. "Obviously I wasn't hiding, but merely checking to make sure the place is habitable."

"I beg your pardon? Of course this place is habitable. It's been used by dozens of productions over the years. Who do you think you are?"

"Aw, come now, Cassie," Mal gently protested. "I'm sure he didn't mean to offend you."

Yeah, judging from the way he was eyeing her, there was nothing to be too sure of there. She crossed her arms. Yes, she might be making a mountain out of the proverbial, but thanks to His Royal Lateness, who apparently couldn't be bothered to tell anyone he'd be delayed, she'd been forced to delay the tour, which meant putting off helping her dad. Her heart panged afresh. Her dad was only getting older, and she hated letting him down. This, along with two phone calls—one involving a burst pipe, the other cancelling their next movie booking in four months, so goodbye financial buffer—meant her patience, never her strongest virtue, was even thinner than normal. Besides, she'd encountered too many guys who thought themselves better than everyone else, like Mark, a high school ex who used to mock her math ability. She'd never had time for arrogance or divas. And everything about this man, from his leather jacket to his tanned face and carefully sculpted hairstyle—how much gel had he used?—screamed arrogant diva. So not her cup of tea.

Still, the fact he'd be on her set for the next four months meant she couldn't afford to let him get under her skin. She drew in a steadying breath. She'd just need to ignore him. She faked a smile and spun on her booted heel, putting her back to Harrison as she beckoned the remaining cast to come inside.

"So, as I was saying before, this building is what we call Harry's Saloon, which must be why certain people seem to want to claim it as their own." She quickly stepped aside, gesturing like a game show host at the man standing behind her.

A trickle of laughter was quickly followed by murmured welcomes and a few hugs from some of the younger cast members. Mostly female, but whatever. Obviously, there was no accounting for taste. Ainsley Beckett, Cassie noticed, only offered a smile and a greeting, like it didn't matter that her brand-new co-star was late.

But come on. One of the main reasons Cassie was conducting this tour at all was to help the newcomers familiarize themselves with the set. Mr. Nonchalant over there hadn't even properly apologized for wasting people's time. Who did he think he was? Leonardo Di Caprio?

Harrison cleared his throat. "I'm very sorry for being late. Please forgive me. It certainly wasn't my intention to waste anyone's time today."

Hmm.

"Anyway, as you can see, this saloon has a more rustic feel than some of the other places we've already seen today." She shot a look at Harrison. "Most of us, anyway."

His lips buckled in on each other, and he glanced away.

Good. He should feel bad. "So we've now seen most of the buildings where most of the shooting for the main scenes will take place, which leaves some of the on-site accommodation." Cassie gestured for Lance Fidler to take the lead.

"Thanks, Cassie. It's always good to have that refresher. So, regarding accommodation, this year we're switching things up and doing things a little differently..."

Cassie pressed her lips together, her gaze sliding to Harrison. His gaze instantly flicked away. Huh. Had he been watching her? Just wait until he heard what Lance was going to say.

"...and so, in addition to our usual trailers, thanks to our wonderful ranch hosts, we'll also have a limited number of on-site opportunities for those who want a full experience of what life could be like back in the day."

Harrison guffawed. "Are you serious?"

"Deadly."

So it didn't look like he'd be putting up his hand to stay in the western town's apartments any time soon. Well, good. This year's opportunity to increase revenue by expanding their in-town accommodation could do without the likes of him.

Harrison whistled, smirking a little as he shook his head. "I know some people here think they're getting into the role simply by dressing the part..." His cold eyes glanced at her. "But don't you think that's overkill?"

She frowned at him. Wait. Did he think she was part of the crew?

Mal now wore his own crease between his brows. "I would think you'd be trying to do all you could to fit in, Harrison. Not looking for excuses."

Ouch. She snuck another peek at him, catching his wince which he quickly hid. "I don't mean to sound like I'm making excuses."

Except he was. So far today he'd blamed her "poor directions" for being late, and now he was complaining about having to get into character. Honestly. The man needed to grow up and take some responsibility.

Her phone buzzed in her back pocket. She checked the number, nodded to Mal, then took Lance aside. "I need to return this call, but if there's any questions, you'll know where I'll be."

"Thanks, Cass. The place looks great as always."

"I'm glad you approve." Her gaze drifted to the arms-crossed actor nearby, who clearly didn't approve. Well, too bad. He'd signed on the dotted line which meant he was supposed to be here. He'd have to work on his attitude to make sure the next four months weren't all pain.

"Excuse me," she murmured, flashing Ainsley a grin, who offered one of her own, before Cassie headed outside.

Then she returned the call. "Hello, Mr. Cameron? This is Cassie James from Three Creek Ranch Western Town. You just called us about our movie set..."

Cassie groaned as she dragged herself up the steps and inside the ranch house, then paused in the back doorway as familiar, well-loved aromas nearly brought her to her knees. She'd joked about her mom's hippie tendencies before, but the woman sure knew her way around a stove. She lingered, inhaling the comfort of this place that looked and smelled a lot like love. After the day she had, she needed more of that.

"Cassie?"

She turned and straightened. "Hannah!"

After a hug hello, Cassie turned to her brother who swept her up in his own strong hug. "I might've known if Hannah was here you'd not be too far away," she teased.

"This is my home too, sis." He ruffled her hair affectionately.

Well, it was sometimes. The man had an apartment in the city, but like Dorothy from a certain movie, all the James family knew there was no place like home.

Hannah grinned. "And I might be here to talk wedding details with you, but I get the feeling that someone is trying to make the most of our time together now the season is over."

Franklin's and Calgary's hockey season, but whatever. The Stanley Cup was still going. She hoped a Canadian team would raise the Cup this year, and the way Vancouver was going, they might just do that.

"I understand." Cassie glanced at her brother. "He's always been needy."

"Sure have," Franklin said, wrapping Hannah in a hug before giving her a big smooch. "And now I need to get married."

Hmm. Judging from that kiss they probably did.

But that wasn't a thought she cared to pursue, even if the sight of the two of them, so at ease with each other and knee-deep in love, drew a pang of longing for something similar for herself. Not that she'd met any men recently she'd like to explore such things with. In fact, the last new man she'd met—a certain leading man on a certain TV show—was about the last man on earth she'd ever want touching her lips.

She left them to it, then slowly moved to the kitchen. Thinking of what she didn't have never worked well for her. She didn't like herself much when she spiraled into negativity, so it was best to focus on good things instead. Good things, like— "Mom."

Her mother looked up from the oven tray, her glasses fogged up, which drew Cassie's smile. She gave her mom a moment to recover, then hugged her, savoring the comfort.

"Cassie?" Her mom drew back. "Is everything okay?"

She nodded, pasting on a smile, but knew her mom wasn't fooled. Still, with her younger sisters bouncing in, and Franklin and Hannah entering the kitchen, now wasn't the time to talk. Not that there was much to say, anyway.

Jessica groaned, slumping at the table. "Oh my gosh. I don't know how many cats I've seen today. Is a vet allowed to say she much prefers working with dogs than cats?"

"This vet is," Dad said, patting her on the back.

Jess briefly smiled. "I don't know why they were all so hissy today, either."

"Having hissy fits, huh?" Franklin asked.

Jess swapped looks with Cassie. "Someone must be feeling relaxed if he can make bad jokes like that, right?"

"It probably means that he can start helping more with the wedding prep." Hannah poked her fiancé in the side.

Cassie lifted her water glass. "Amen."

The meal of pot roast and vegetables passed as it usually did, with compliments to the chef (Mom) and chief gravy maker (Dad), and exchanges about people's days.

Poppy, her youngest sister, wasn't loving her work at a Calgary dance studio. "But I'm grateful to have a job, even if it's not like it used to be, back when I worked with Bailey in Winnipeg."

"Remind me what you did there?" Hannah asked.

"After Bails and I finished our training, I stayed in Winnipeg and worked for a time, then she and I ran her studio. It was fun. She's really sweet."

Franklin smiled. "I should see if she and Luc Blanchard could meet."

Poppy scoffed. "I can't see that working. Bails isn't exactly a fan of a mullet."

"A mullet?" Mom asked.

"You know, Mom. That men's eighties' hairstyle where it's business at the top, party at the back," Jess said.

"And not just men. I've seen some women wear it too." Poppy's nose wrinkled. "But I don't think he's the kind of guy she needs. He's just too different from her."

"What about opposites who attract?" Jess asked.

"And they're probably not too different. Isn't she a Christian?" Franklin asked. "Luc sure is, so it's not out of the question."

"Bails is a believer. But I think you have to have more in common than just faith." Poppy shrugged.

Sure did. Shared interests, shared goals in life, a shared sense of humor all helped knit people together, even if faith was the most important thing. Cassie slowly scooped up the last of her mashed potatoes. Judging from what she'd seen from Harrison today— arriving late, then hiding, then blaming others and not taking responsibility for his conduct—suggested he was lacking in any sense of accountability, and certainly wasn't indicative of a man of faith. She choked.

"You okay there, sis?" Franklin asked, banging her on the back.

She nodded, snatching up a glass of water and downing it carefully. Great. Now all eyes were on her. And she had zero desire to talk about her day. Or the man who she really didn't want to be thinking about.

Hannah's smile dipped as she glanced at Cassie. "You've been awfully quiet. How was your day?"

Darn. Now that she'd eaten all her food and finished her water she didn't have an easy excuse not to talk. "It was a day."

Hannah's face softened in sympathy. "That good, huh?"

Yep. After her run-in with Harrison this morning, she'd needed to fix the leaking pipe in the dining hall. Fortunately, some of the production crew had proved more than happy to help her, but the taped-up pipe didn't look very professional. At least it worked. She'd returned at lunchtime to overhear Harrison complain that his coffee wasn't hot enough. And while she was tempted to think him a diva, it might well be because the pipes hadn't worked properly yet, which was ultimately her fault, so it only added to her pressure.

Following that, she'd needed to check in with the horse wranglers, in the purpose-built stables for horses used in productions, to discover some of the stalls weren't built quite to code, which had demanded her fixing things all afternoon. And this was day one! Still, the ranch needed the money, and she wasn't about to admit to her lack of competency. Dad didn't need that, anyway. "If it's all the same to you, I'd prefer not to talk about it."

"Oh, honey." Her mother paused from cleaning up.

Dad's chair creaked as he sat back. "Wasn't today the start of the new filming of *As The Heart Draws*?"

She lifted a shoulder in a half-shrug. "They arrived, but won't start filming for another day or so."

"Was Ainsley there?" Poppy asked.

Cassie nodded. "She's always the first cast member on set. Such a professional."

"And so pretty, too." Poppy sighed. "I hope this year she and her Mountie finally get married."

Cassie kept her face as Sphinx-like as she could. No way could she admit the truth.

"Anyone new we should keep an eye out for?" Jess asked, knowing full well that Cassie couldn't explain. That didn't stop her asking. Every. Single. Season.

Cassie pressed her lips together, as her heart twanged in protest.

"Ooh, that face says there is." Poppy laughed. "That's it. I'm skipping classes tomorrow to find out who it is."

"Lincoln Cash isn't back, is he?" Jess asked.

"Last I heard he's involved with someone in Muskoka," Hannah said.

Good. Change the subject time. "You know the most interesting things." Cassie faced her soon-to-be sister-in-love. "How was your day?"

"Good." Hannah smiled. "But don't think you can get us off topic that easily."

"She fits in so well, doesn't she?" Franklin said, kissing Hannah's cheek.

"Actually, I think the reason you're here is so we can finalize a few more wedding details, am I right? And I still have more work to do," Cassie said. A number of emails needed attention, then after that she really needed her sleep. "So we should really get started."

"Fair enough." Hannah's expression held more than a drop of smirk. "But don't think we're not interested."

"Yes, Ms. Reporter. We know."

Not that there was any story here for Hannah or anyone else to sniff out. Because there wasn't. It didn't matter that Harrison or anyone else had arrived in her town today. She wasn't interested in him, and he'd made it plain he didn't like her at all. But she had a feeling that keeping a lid on her family's curiosity would be easier said than done.

UNFAMILIAR NIGHT SOUNDS crept past the window. Creaks. Chirrups. A humming kind of moan. And while he was pretty sure that last sound was an air conditioner, he wasn't completely certain. Part of the reason why he didn't like the country was that you never could trust it. There were always things out there trying to get him, whether it be bugs or unseen cow patties or wildfires. Not that he'd had experience with the latter, but still, the fact remained. The country was filled with unpleasant surprises.

He shifted as he glanced up from his iPad, and the trailer creaked slightly. Why the cast had to stay on site was a mystery. Mal and Lance had said it was good for cast and crew bonding, but Harrison wasn't so sure. Surely it wouldn't be so bad for him to stay at one of Calgary's hotels another night. It didn't even have to be the Hilton. But the wise heads in charge probably decided that renting a trailer for several months was cheaper, which was why he was here, and not there. And since Ainsley was staying as well, and appeared perfectly happy with the arrangement, it didn't seem like he had any room to complain.

He sighed. The trailer was decked out with all the usual modern conveniences, and after viewing the town's "accommodation" the trailer looked a darn sight better than the little apartments scattered through the town's buildings. He wanted some link to modernity as well as a good-sized bed, rather than those antiquated things that looked straight from *Little House on the Prairie*. At least here he had internet service, even if it was a little spotty.

A groan escaped, his legs and backside protesting the exercise he'd been forced to endure. After the town walk, some of the cast had undergone horse riding "refresher" training, and he worked with the show's riding expert to improve his posture. Ainsley hadn't required corrective instruction. He was half tempted to go seek her out, but she'd made it clear she wanted an early night. Which seemed weird when they were all forced to stay on-site for cast bonding and the leading lady wasn't around, but whatever. Nearly all of them knew each other, while he was the newbie, so probably he was the one who had to make the biggest effort to fit in.

A knock came on his trailer's door. "Hey Harrison? You coming?"

He didn't recognize the voice, but did the intention, so that meant a "Yeah."

He pulled himself upright, then staggered to the door, swinging it open, then gingerly walked down the metal steps. Murmurs drew his feet to a group of chairs, positioned around a small campfire. Huh. So it really was kind of like back in the olden days, like they'd be portraying.

"Howdy." He smirked at himself. Well, look who was going all cowboy. Even if it was a Mountie he'd portray. Man. He was getting as bad as that cowgirl-wannabe production assistant who'd walked them around the town this morning. The one who'd clobbered him in the shoulder when he'd startled her this morning. It was kinda weird he hadn't seen her again. But then, this was a large production, with lots of crew, and while he was trying to remember people's names he couldn't quite remember everyone.

"So how are you settling in?" his co-star Dustin Trooper— now there was a Mountie-sounding name if ever he'd heard one— asked.

"It's all good." Well, he hoped it would be. Provided the coffee was hotter tomorrow. His gut tensed, regret kneading within at how he'd acted earlier. He didn't like to complain—he was pretty sure that cowgirl assistant had overheard him and was adding that to his list of crimes and misdemeanors—but a man needed caffeine. And it was always best to start the way you meant to go on. Set your expectations high, and all that, so others could meet them. There was no point being a pushover, and resenting others simply because you didn't speak up. Like his mom used to do.

His insides tensed as they always did whenever he thought of her. He tossed a smile at the others to hide it, but they weren't looking at him. Instead, their heads were all lifted to the heavens above, like they'd never seen a night sky before. And well, fair enough. He was happy to forget the past and focus on the now. He'd never seen a sky with quite so many stars before, either. Maybe there were some good things about the country, after all.

He tilted back his chin, too. "Sure can see the stars well out here."

"We always love coming to the ranch," Dana Drewe, Ainsley's character's friend, said. "It's so peaceful and relaxing, like you really are slipping back into the past. I have to admit coming here is the highlight of my year."

Wow. Her life must be real exciting.

"I suspect plenty of us would think the same," Dustin said, his gaze dropping to Harrison. "Good to have you here as part of the family." He held up his mug. "Welcome."

Aww. Now wasn't that sweet? "It's great to be here."

And suddenly, like hearing the words spoken aloud had felled scales from his eyes, it was.

It *was* nice to be in an environment like this, where people were relaxed and welcoming. He'd been on plenty of sets where competition and envy were the name of the game. His time on *As The Heart Draws* had shown none of that. Of course, it was super early in the shoot still, but from all of the interactions he'd witnessed everyone appeared to get on really well. Well, apart from Ms. Cowboy Hat this morning.

"Hey, pardon the newbie question, but who was the chick leading the town tour this morning?"

Dana's teeth glinted in the darkness. "You mean Cassie?"

"If she's the one with the cowboy hat, then yeah. I haven't seen her since."

Dustin's laughter rumbled. "Oh, you'll be seeing her. Cassie is always on set, one way or the other."

Hmm. Sounded annoying.

"She's what I like to call a good-value woman. You can trust her to do what she says," Dana said.

Uh huh. Trust her not to go out of her way to welcome a

newcomer, that was for sure. What kind of person went all kung-fu and slammed a door into a man? She was lucky he wasn't suing her. Although, maybe it was the tiniest bit impressive how she'd stood up for herself like his mom never had, but no man liked feeling like a fool or a coward. What had he been thinking, hiding behind a door like a child? Ugh. Considering these guys hadn't exactly been privy to what had gone on before in the saloon, he wasn't about to advertise his inadequacies. Well, they'd likely already seen him on a horse and now knew some of his shortcomings, but there was no need to add to any disenchantment.

"Yeah, she's great. Nothing is too much trouble for her—"

Except for being nice to newcomers on set, maybe.

"—so if ever you have any problems, you can always talk to her."

Yeah, no thanks. Silence stretched, and he realized they were waiting for him to respond. But he couldn't say what he really felt, especially with them singing her praises like she personally had placed each star above. "Sounds like she's, uh, committed to the cause."

"That she is," Dana said with a half-smile, her look full of curiosity.

Okay, so maybe he'd been a bit obvious in his dislike. Way to go with the no negativity vibe he'd hoped to portray. He offered a quick smile back then studied his Skechers.

"Imagine getting to live here." Dustin exhaled. "Some people have all the luck, eh?"

Whoa. Dustin knew this wasn't real, right? Sure, there were ranches nearby, and he supposed people actually had to live on those ranches, but it wasn't like this was an actual place where one could live and have a Hollywood career. It might be thirty minutes to Calgary—or more like an hour if one had bad directions—but it was still way too remote to live long-term.

Actually living here would mean few amenities. No Uber-eats or Door Dash for food delivery. The sounds of cows bellowing every waking hour. Unfamiliar sounds. Hazards like snakes.

Imagine the hike if you ran out of milk. Thirty minutes might not be the same as the hours it might take some people in deepest darkest Montana to reach civilization, but it was plenty far enough for him, thank you very much. Although, maybe running out of milk wasn't a problem on a ranch. Or did that mean they ran beef cattle, and would never run out of steak?

His lips twisted, as new appreciation filled him for what the pioneers had to face, and understanding grew for why Mal and the team had insisted the cast stay on site. Living here, sitting under the stars, might give only a glimpse of what the pioneers had to face, but he could understand a little more what it would've been like in those days. A man couldn't live isolated like he could now. People were important. Community was vital. People needed each other, relied on each other. And just as he relied on the riding instructor to help him with his horsemanship, so this cast and crew relied on Harrison to do his job and bring his best. Which meant sucking down the negativity that was all too quick to pounce.

"So, this Cassie chick. Does she always go around in a cowboy hat?"

"Usually." Dana peered at him across the top of her mug. "Why?"

He shrugged. "I just wondered if all the crew were mandated to dress in western gear."

Dustin shrugged. "Makes sense to me. If you're out in the sun a lot, why wouldn't you wear a hat?"

"I guess." But a fringed jacket, cowboy boots, the whole she-bang? Screamed wannabe to him.

He stayed a few more minutes, enjoying the night sounds. From somewhere in the distance he could hear a cow mooing. Somewhere else a bird sang. The hush of cooler breeze rasped against his bristly cheek, found the back of his neck which had been freshly shaved. The production's barber had been tasked with the job of making their hairstyles as period-appropriate as possible, which meant a number of men were looking a little more historically accurate than earlier today.

Another dance of coolness drew his shiver. Bedtime called. He pushed to his feet. Offered a smile. "Well, nice to hang. I guess I better go hit the hay." Oh, look at him with the clichés.

Dana chuckled. "Good night, cowboy."

"That's Special Constable Fraser to you, young lady."

Dustin's laughter joined Dana's, and Harrison grinned and tipped his imaginary hat at them both, before wending his way through the trailers to his own.

Home, for the next four months. Awesome.

He made a quick pit stop at the amenities, brushed his teeth, then got into bed. At least the sheets felt fresh and cool.

He plugged in his phone and checked it one last time. Imagine a time when there were no phones, and the only thing a man had was his thoughts. Thank God they didn't live in those days now.

He checked the numbers that Maxine had given him. Then checked his social media, relieved to see his recent post about "a secret new project" was getting plenty of likes and comments. Richard had made it clear that part of the reason the producers wanted Harrison on board was because they thought he'd bring a younger audience. He hoped his posts would stir up interest and intrigue and add to that.

So he'd drop a few clues over the next month, until the *As the Heart Draws* current season finale had dropped, and people needed a new drawcard once they realized Tanner Pearson wasn't returning.

Heartthrob was a funny hat to wear. Harrison had always been the side-kick, so progressing to leading man was an honor, if somewhat daunting. He wondered how the Brad Pitts or Lincoln Cash-caliber actors managed, always being photographed or judged on what they were wearing or who they were with. An actor might prefer the top billing and paycheck that came with the title of heartthrob, but it had a downside too. Any woman he was ever seen with was his latest girlfriend. If he dared to be seen out at night with her it was assumed they were sleeping together. It was partly why he didn't go out with girls as much these days, as he didn't want them to experience the level of harassment he'd occasionally been subjected to. Going out with Marcia, his most recent ex, had been okay, seeing she was as hungry as he was to reach the next rung in the ladder of fame. That relationship had been more for show than for anything real. Once he'd realized she was more into using him for her career rather than him it'd been a weight off, as they lacked any genuine connection. He hadn't exactly pursued anyone since. Of course, not going out with women meant some people assumed he leant the other way, which wasn't true at *all*.

And while some people assumed the worst, others thought his roles meant he was like the characters he played. After his time on *Beach Guard*, his agent had steered him to roles that were never too spicy, so his reputation meant the role of a morally upright constable now fit well, and wouldn't be too far off his fans' expectations. But that led to its own challenges, and fears that people would now forever pigeonhole him as only worthy of playing meek, nice guys. He wasn't nearly as nice as some of his roles had made him out to be. Blurring the line between fact and fiction was something fans couldn't always understand.

He closed his eyes. Exhaled slowly. Deep breath in, hold two, three. Let it out, two, three, four. And again. He really needed sleep.

Somewhere between restlessness and sleep he caught glimpses of the ranch, the hills, the vast openness of this place, and he drifted into dreaming about what Constable Fraser would have faced, had this fictitious story proved true. He knew *As The Heart Draws* was based on a famous Canadian author's memoirs, so maybe it wasn't so far-fetched after all.

He could try to channel the real man his character was based on. He could perhaps be the hero, save the girl, save the day. Be the tough guy his dad had never believed him capable of being. Prove him wrong. Win the plaudits, win the praise.

Memories tiptoed in. His dad's words, worming inside: *You should never have been born. You're such a girl. You're a mistake. Loser. Diva.*

Memories of the fights, the arguments, the punches. Times when he'd cowered, just like his mom, helpless against his dad's drunken rages. Wishing he was stronger. Wishing he could've protected his mom. Wishing he was braver. He didn't need his therapist to explain why he was drawn to playing tough guy roles.

A creaking sound stole him awake. He squinted in the darkness, but could see nothing out of the ordinary. He closed his eyes again, imagining lifting a trophy and shoving it in his dad's face and forcing him to realize that acting was a legitimate career choice as much as investment banking, and just because a man had a head for numbers didn't mean he could also have a heart for storytelling too.

A rustling sound snapped his eyes open again. Then the cabin of his trailer echoed with his scream.

Three

The sound drew Cassie's focus from the peace of the first soft golden lift of dawn to nudge Ginger to a gallop. Something was wrong. She cantered down the hill overlooking where the trailers were parked, relieved to see the security guard was awake and was hurrying to a lit-up trailer where she presumed the sound had come from. What had happened? This was terrible. How many other things would go wrong—and they hadn't even started filming yet?

One of the trailers' doors was flung open, and a figure staggered out in boxers. She blinked. Okay.

Wait. She squinted. Was that Mr. Grumble-bum from yesterday? Her lips lifted on one side. Had that been him screaming? Or —she frowned—someone else? As the person responsible for the site, she needed to find out.

She directed Ginger to the trailer compound and tied her to a wooden fence rail, then hurried to the trailer that had its lights on. Fortunately, it didn't seem like others had been disturbed, although why the others had stayed asleep while she heard the cry for help was a mystery.

A rumble of low voices drew her then she stumbled to a pause. Up close, Harrison Woods, in almost all his glory, was certainly a sight to behold for a woman who had never seen a naked man. Not that he was naked, exactly. Thank goodness he wore boxers.

His gaze pivoted to her, then his jaw sagged. "You."

"Me." She smiled.

Today's security guard—Chuck—coughed. "You might want to put some clothes on, Mr. Woods."

"What happened?" she asked, pointedly not looking at the actor, who quickly disappeared back inside the trailer.

Was that a smile on Chuck's face? It couldn't be all bad if he was smiling, could it?

"I, um, think it's all under control now."

"Was it him screaming?" she asked in a low voice, gesturing toward the trailer. "Or was that someone else?"

Now that was definitely a smile. Her heart eased a smidge.

"It was him," Chuck confirmed. "It appears a small creature might've been responsible."

"What?"

No. Not a mouse. She sure hoped he didn't mean a mouse. The trailers might be rented but she couldn't afford for any mice to get into the props barn and wreak havoc like they had three years ago. Too many costumes and soft furnishings had needed tossing then replacing, and she had no interest in a repeat. Apart from the heartbreaking damage and sheer grossness factor of cleaning, the business might not survive too many financial hits like that. Besides, as the person managing the site, she'd always felt a sense of responsibility for things running smoothly while any production was on Three Creek land.

Chuck's soft snickers quieted. "A mouse."

She sighed. *Lord, keep my props safe*. "Let me guess: he doesn't like mice."

"No, I don't."

Her gaze swerved up to where Harrison now wore a t-shirt and jeans. She bit her lip. His t-shirt was on inside out. "Are you okay now?"

"I wasn't scared," he insisted.

"Of course not," she said soothingly.

His eyes narrowed, and she had to bite back laughter. Chuck wasn't so circumspect, his renewed barely-smothered chuckles drawing another look of annoyance from the show's new hero.

Aww, bless him. She'd never met a man who was frightened by a mouse. Her dad sure wasn't, and she'd bet if Franklin met one he'd simply clobber it with a hockey stick and call it done. Good thing her brother was marrying Hannah and not someone with overly developed animal-loving sensibilities like Jess.

"Do you need me to come inside and check for you?" she asked, as innocently as she could.

"I bet you'd like that, wouldn't you?"

She ignored his insinuation, keeping her smile sweet. "No, not at all. I just don't want you to get the wrong idea about things here."

He muttered something she couldn't quite hear.

"Alright then. I'll take that as a no." She backed away.

His bicep bulged as he rubbed a hand over his face, his cheeks bristly in a morning look some might call sexy. Not that she thought him attractive. He was much too grouchy at this time of day to be appealing. He frowned at her. "What are you doing around here anyway at this time? The sun hasn't even risen yet."

"Actually..." She pointed to the golden-hued horizon.

He made a face, mumbling something else she guessed wasn't complimentary—about the early hour or herself, she didn't care to know.

"I'm an early bird. We tend to get the worm."

He yawned. "I sure don't plan on getting worms while I'm here."

She chuckled, and he appeared to realize what he said, as his cheeks pinked. "I mean—"

"I know what you meant." Was it un-Christian of her to enjoy watching him squirm? This day kept getting better and better. "Well, are you definitely okay to go back to sleep now?"

"You want to hold my hand and make sure?" he grouched.

Yeah, that'd be a solid "no."

He turned, and the way the shirt clung to him she could count his abs. If she'd been a different kind of woman she might take a mental picture. But because she wasn't that kind of woman, she looked away. "Alright then. If you're sure you'll be okay."

"I'm not a child," he snapped.

"Of course you're not."

His gaze lasered into hers in a look that said he was very much not amused by her tone. She swallowed a smile. She hadn't meant to sound patronizing. Well, not much, anyway.

If his eyes narrowed anymore they might shut. Which might be good for all concerned. "I'll let you get back to sleep now, then shall I?" She nodded to Chuck. "Have fun with that."

"Yes, ma'am."

Her lips quirked, and she hurried back to Ginger, untying her. Well, if she needed confirmation, there it was. The show's big handsome hero was afraid of mice. And was definitely not a morning person. He couldn't be more opposite to her if he tried.

She moved to where sounds from the dining hall suggested the cooks were already up and preparing breakfast. Most of the cast and crew would take another hour before they would wake, but days like today with predicted fine weather meant it was important for people to make the most of the daylight hours while they could. She went inside.

"Hey Ms. James!" Annie Hunter, the production's chief cook, beamed at her.

"Mornin'." Cassie grinned. She did love a person who appreciated an early start like she did.

"Usual?"

"Please."

Annie moved to the coffee pot and poured Cassie a cup. "I haven't had a chance to get the fixings out yet."

"I know where it all is." Cassie drew out the plastic tub of creamers and sweetener varieties and placed them on the table next to where Annie hefted the coffee urn. Real milk and real cream would come out when the first of the real crew straggled in. "I hope the pipes are all still working?"

"You did good, hon. It's all working as it should be."

Phew. "Thank You, God."

"Amen," Annie agreed. "We don't want no more complaints about the coffee not being hot enough, now do we?"

"No, ma'am."

"I get the impression a certain somebody is addicted to the stuff."

"Mm-hm."

Annie winked. "Good thing that man is plenty fine to look at, right?"

If you liked your cup of joe with a shot of snarl in the morning. "Sure."

"I mean, Tanner was good-looking and all, but I always felt there was something just a little babyish about his face, like I couldn't quite believe him to be on Ainsley's level. This Harrison, however." She fanned herself. "Holy smokes. The man's got a bit of something something about him, don't you think?"

Cassie swallowed a smile, knowing Annie was just playing, doing her best to get Cassie to bite. Annie was a grandmother, and had been happily married to Ted, the lead horse wrangler, for nearly forty years, and had never been shy about offering her opinions about anything and everything—especially Cassie's love life, or lack thereof. If Annie thought that about Harrison now, she would likely have combusted or melted into a puddle on the spot at the sight Cassie had seen just fifteen minutes earlier.

A cleared throat swung her attention behind. Then her jaw to the floor. She closed it with an audible snap, as Annie chuckled.

"Well, hello handsome. We were just talking about you, weren't we, Miss Cassie?"

He just bet they were. Coming in on the tail-end of a conversation where it was apparent he was the topic of choice was never much fun. At least Ms. Annie thought him okay in the looks department. Miss Cassie, on the other hand, seemed determined not to look at him at all.

Well, good. He pushed down the little internal huff of disappointment—seriously? She didn't think him good-looking?—and nodded to the coffee urn. "Is it ready yet?"

"Sure thing, Sweet Cheeks," Annie answered.

Sweet Cheeks?

He rubbed a hand over his jaw then glanced over at where Miss Cowboy Hat stood, sipping her coffee, watching him like she couldn't believe it was him.

He cocked an eyebrow. "Something wrong?"

"I'm just surprised to see you up. I got the impression before that mornings weren't exactly your thing."

Ah, that. He scratched the back of his neck. "Couldn't sleep."

Her brow puckered. "I hope your visitor didn't return."

"Nope." Thank goodness. How embarrassing had that moment before been? And, conscious that people talked, and he hadn't exactly given off good vibes before, he'd decided he needed to make an effort and appear less wussy than that impression had certainly given .

"Good."

He yawned. Rubbed his face with his hand. "Do you get many critters around here?"

"This is the country. Critters are part of the deal."

His lip curled. "That's why I like the city."

"Each to their own." She sipped her coffee, her gaze straying to where the cook watched them.

He nodded to her, but it was the cowgirl wannabe's calmness that rankled him. Made him want to puncture it. "I hope the accommodation will improve. That trailer was barely habitable."

"Excuse me?"

"You heard me," he challenged.

"Whoa. You need to calm down. You're acting like a diva."

"I'm not a diva," he snapped.

Her mouth curved.

"I'm not!"

Wait—was she chuckling now? Was this no-name chick actually laughing at him? Who on earth did she think she was? "I don't know who you think you are, but your attitude is definitely not appreciated right now."

"Right back atcha, mister."

Mister? Did she seriously not recognize him? Wow.

He turned, poured himself a cup of joe, hating how early starts made him snarly and less able to shrug off the echo of his dad's opinion. He wasn't weak. He wasn't a diva. He just needed caffeine, stat. Enough to drown the echoes of the past.

By now some of the crew were wandering in, and he was forced to exchange greetings, to pretend he loved getting up with the sun. The coffee was good, made the synapses work in his brain, so he might get a redemption round after the horrific start.

He glanced back at the cowgirl. Her lips tilted for a second as she eyed him over her cup, then she nodded, her hat slipping slightly.

Honestly, what was the deal with her cowboy hat? His gaze trickled down her attire, to her collared long-sleeved pink shirt, jeans and boots, like an advertisement for Wranglers. Wasn't she just a production assistant? Why did she dress like she thought she was Annie Oakley?

"You know your shirt is on inside out?" the cook said to him.

Harrison peered down, pulled out the reverse image. Man. So it was. He glanced up quickly, caught Miss Cassie smooth away a smile. Wait—had it been inside out earlier too? This day was going from bad to worse.

Still, this was something he could fix now. He tugged off his shirt, heard a wolf whistle from the cook, and caught a glimpse of

Miss Cassie's wide eyes before she pivoted away. Aww. Was she shy? He was half tempted to brazen it out and give her a good eyeful of his pecs, then realized it had been a long time since he'd met a woman who averted her eyes. Which was actually not a bad thing. He didn't want to come across as a tool, even though it was probably too late for that. Especially with that particular move.

"Am I late for the party?" One of his female co-stars asked, smirking as she entered the room.

"I'll leave you all to it," Cowgirl Cassie mumbled, her cheeks still pink as she hurried away.

He watched her exit, feeling ten shades of fool, when a cough swung his attention back to the actress. He frowned. What was her—?

"You can't remember my name, can you, Harrison?"

He winced. How he loved it when someone called him out on that while proving they remembered his. "I'm sorry. There was a lot going on yesterday."

"Dana."

"Hey."

Dana waggled her eyebrows. She had to be about his age. "So, can we expect breakfast and a show each morning?"

He coughed. "No."

She laughed, and a second later Annie joined in, leaving him feeling even more foolish than before. Good thing the cowgirl wasn't still here.

He shuffled to the coffee cart, tempted to stomp, but figured that wasn't about to win him any favors, either. Then he mumbled a goodbye and hurried out the door.

Outside, the air held a heavy quality, like the weight of dew. He usually preferred never to see this time of day, and in his life had been blessed with only a handful of necessary pre-dawn arrivals on set. But here, there was something about the light, the way it appeared to hold new promise, that meant maybe he'd been missing a thing or two. And maybe having a mouse wake him from his slumber wasn't the worst thing that could've happened.

He moved to the fence, then glanced along the wooden rail and recognized the blonde-brown braid hanging under the white hat. Then cringed. It was bad enough to have proved his complete wimpishness this morning, squealing like a little kid over a stupid mouse. It was quite enough to then follow up that routine with his failure of a shirtless moment. Clearly, she hadn't liked what she'd seen. Either time. He was half tempted to apologize—obviously they'd gotten off on the wrong foot— but something held him back. Pride, probably. It was a good thing she was only a lowly production assistant and not someone with any real clout. Imagine if she was connected to Mal.

Still, the thought she wasn't into ogling him, her manner in complete contrast to the two women inside, and Marcia before them, intrigued him. Miss Cassie certainly didn't lack confidence or courage, judging from the slammed door of yesterday. And, now he thought about it, he actually could kind of understand why a woman would act in that way. He must've looked a little suspect, hiding in the shadows like a criminal. So, yeah, okay, respect for standing up for herself instead of being like his mom. And it wasn't her fault he'd been late. So her actions were perhaps justified, and maybe he did owe her an apology after all. Because she clearly thought him weird, and while he was definitely not your average dude, and originating from Portland he'd always happily own a little weird, he didn't want her thinking him as more off than merely slightly odd.

He glanced back at her, and she shifted, almost like she'd been watching him too but hadn't wanted to be seen doing so.

He swallowed the rest of his coffee then moved closer, employing stealth ninja moves that might've once made an appearance on a kids' TV show a million years ago, back when he'd been green and looking for his break and willing to dress in cringy costumes on a show he now sure hoped nobody would ever see.

She didn't move, her gaze fixed on the sunrise, as if lost in its beauty, one arm loosely over the wooden paling as he crept closer. Then he cleared his throat.

And she yelped and spun around, her coffee flying from her cup and landing on his chest.

"Ahh!"

She jumped back, one hand over her mouth, eyes wide with shock. "I'm so sorry!"

He peeled his t-shirt away from his skin with a wince, thankful her coffee had cooled and was only tepid in temperature.

"Are you alright?" she asked.

"I'll survive." Although this top wouldn't, and would likely never be white again. Which was a shame, as it fitted really well, and he'd picked it up on a trip to Mexico so it wasn't exactly easy to re-purchase. Still, he couldn't blame her for her reaction. At least she hadn't bashed him with a hunk of wood like she had with the door last time. "I shouldn't have snuck up on you." Wait, said like that, just made him sound like a stalker. "I mean—"

"So why did you?" She balanced her mug on top of the wooden fencepole and faced him.

Good question. How to explain he didn't want to interrupt her moment of peace? "I, uh, didn't want to disturb you?"

"And look how well that turned out."

Hmm. In his career, he hadn't come across too many production assistants so skilled in the sarcasm department. Weren't they supposed to be nice to the cast?

She fisted her hips, her chin tilting. "Look, I don't know what your problem is, but I don't appreciate men skulking around, sneaking up on people or hiding. That just makes you look strange. Normal people don't do that."

"Normal is overrated." And no actors he knew could ever lay claim to that. Creatives couldn't be boxed into whatever counted as "normal" these days.

She blew out a breath, and looked away at the horizon.

From this distance, he could appreciate how the sun gilded her hair, carving her silhouette in bronze and shadows.

She faced him. "I think it's best if you stay away from me."

Wow. Really? He shoved his hands in his pockets. Jerked his chin. "Probably safest for me. Who knows what you'll do next time?"

"Me? I'm not the one acting weird. That's all you."

He had no comeback. Except, "Some people obviously bring it out of me."

Her eyes narrowed, and he could almost see the steam pouring from her ears. Then she surprised him by thrusting out her hand.

He eyed it. This felt like a trick, something else with the potential to go wrong. "What?"

"You and me."

His heart stuttered. No way in Hades, lady. "You want a truce?"

"Get real. I want you to promise to leave me alone, and I'll do the same."

"Now that's a promise I can keep," he muttered. Except, "Don't you work here?"

"Yes, but don't let that stop you."

"Fine, then." He grasped her hand. Felt a strange warm current zip up his arm from their clasped palms. So he dropped it. He couldn't afford to think like that. Not with this she-devil of a woman. "Well, I guess it's time for me to go change this shirt you ruined."

Her face softened for a moment. "I hope you didn't get burned. It *was* an accident."

He knew that, but it still didn't stop his mouth from projectile-vomiting more snark. "Sure it was."

"It was!"

"Well, if it makes you feel any better, I'll live. Probably."

Her lips pressed together.

He bit back his amusement at her obvious frustration. "See you around, Miss Cassie."

"Not if I can help it," she muttered, then pivoted on her booted heel and walked away.

. . .

THE REST of his day passed in breakfast, costume fittings, blocking scenes, running lines. Mal had promised they'd start filming tomorrow, and his character's role meant he'd be in most of the filming. It'd stay that way over the first few weeks, as much of the interest would be in the new character and the new dynamics that would have to be established, especially with poor grieving widow Abigail, the character played by Ainsley. His introduction into the series would involve literally charging into town on a white horse—a sign as old as the hills that he was one of the good guys. But fortunately, that opening scene of the first episode wouldn't be filmed for a few more weeks, which allowed for more of the interpersonal dialogue between himself and Ainsley.

As they ran lines, he was once again struck by what a professional Ainsley was. She knew her lines already while he was still struggling.

"Put it down to an early start," he mumbled, when he'd fluffed his line for the fifth time.

"I heard you were up at the crack of dawn."

He yawned as if her words reminded his brain what had happened this morning. "Not by choice."

"Not an early bird, huh?"

"Nope." Unlike a certain woman who definitely preferred that time of day. What was wrong with her? At least she'd kept her promise and he'd had nothing more to do with her today. He'd seen her in the distance once, but she was doing a great job of steering clear of him while he did the same.

Regret chased him. He didn't want to be someone people chose to avoid. He didn't want to be like his dad in any way shape or form. Hence no drinking. No mooching off others. No hitting a woman or kid. The fact he might've inherited the worst of both his mom and dad's traits stung. He wasn't like that. He'd do anything to prove them wrong.

He finally managed to get his lines right, and Mal soon pronounced himself satisfied, then they were released for the day. He was sorely tempted to snatch a few minutes sleep, but figured that'd probably mess with his sleep cycles later, so he forced himself to stay awake through dinner and an hour of post-meal conversation. But his early start soon had him done for, and he made his excuses, showered, and went to his trailer.

He hoped Maxine had dealt with the mouse, and the trailer had been deep-cleaned as promised. It looked tidier and certainly smelled better, but who knew if that had actually done the job? He needed to get to sleep. Stat. And a full night's sleep at that. He couldn't afford another day feeling like his brain cells were operating through sludge.

After staggering to his bed, and checking the linens thoroughly—everything smelled fresh, as Maxine had promised—he got in, half wondering if he should have put on shorts and a t-shirt as well, just in case another early morning interruption occurred. No way did he want a repeat of this morning, and end up embarrassing anyone—or himself—with his night wear or lack thereof. At least he'd been wearing boxers.

He plugged in his phone, put it aside, then switched off the light. The phone's charging mode sent a thin spear of orange light through the dark.

For some reason it made him think of that moment early this morning when the sun's glow on the horizon had stolen through his embarrassment, reminding him not all was pain and trouble. And while today had held its share of highs and lows, tomorrow was always a new day.

He closed his eyes. Preferably, it would be a day without any further embarrassing moments with the wannabe cowgirl.

Four

Cassie lassoed the steer and directed it to the gate where her father waited. Once upon a time she'd had fun entering rodeos and had even scored cash prizes for her skills in breakaway and tied-down calf roping. These days she was always too busy.

"Thanks, Cass. He's a stubborn one, this one."

"No problem."

"I mean it. I appreciate your help. Especially when you're so busy, with the TV show and the wedding and all."

She winced. The wedding. She still needed to organize the details for Hannah's girls' night in Calgary this weekend. Was three days long enough? She needed something spectacular and memorable, yet offering a degree of privacy. Something that wasn't crazy expensive, but was still Instagram-worthy for a sports reporter who needed to keep her social media likes coming. She sighed. Looked like Poppy and Jess might need to help her out with some ideas.

Her father peered at her. "You sure you're okay?"

"Yep." Dad didn't need to know any of that. "Now that the show has clicked into gear I'm only checking on prop inventory today, so it's fine. I'll start on that when I'm finished here."

"Okay," her dad said slowly. "But are *you* doing okay?"

She nodded, pasting on a smile. "Nothing to see here."

He studied her. "You were a little distracted last night, that's all."

There was a six-foot-one reason for that. And then the Holy Spirit may have whispered that her conduct wasn't exactly shining a light for Jesus. And while a certain Mountie wannabe had the ability to annoy the snot out of her, it didn't change the fact that God still loved him. Which was just as well, because she sure didn't.

"I'm fine, Dad." And she'd remain fine. Because doing inventory in the prop barn today meant she'd be guaranteed to stay away from the man who pushed her buttons like nobody else had in forever.

After unsaddling Ginger and releasing her to the horse pasture for the day, she went inside the ranch house and kissed her mom on the cheek.

"You're up early," Mom said.

"When am I not?"

After a quick breakfast of cereal and coffee—no way was she taking a chance she might bump into a certain actor again—she checked with her mom about the whereabouts of Miranda.

"I think she's in the barn. Why?"

"I might need her for an inventory check."

Her mom winced. "Not another mouse problem again?"

"I hope not. But if Miranda is there we'll soon know."

She blew her mom a kiss, collected the cat and loaded her in the cat carrier. Miranda had proved the most effective way of dealing with the troubles three years ago. Better than bait which mice ate before hiding in tiny crevices where they died, only to stink up the building, forcing days of arms-aching removal of thousands of items to prevent them from being contaminated. Miranda was a mouser, born and bred for such a task, and as valuable a member of the ranch team as anyone else.

She secured the carrier in the back of her battered old Ford pickup then drove to the prop barn. Part of the arrangement with TV and movie production companies was that they had access to the Three Creek props, many of which were leftovers from companies that hadn't wanted the bother of taking them away. It meant their collection was vast, ranging from everything from period-appropriate furniture and bric-a-brac, to animal skulls (all real), to costumes and footwear and accessories for men, women and children. All in a variety of colors and sizes.

Because *As The Heart Draws* was a repeat customer, many of their costumes for returning cast members were held in a special shipping container, accessed each year by them and nobody else. Their prop department also had a solid idea of how they'd like to dress the sets, which meant they'd already checked out much of what they required. Rather than the tedium of arranging the rental of individual items, she'd organized a general fee for this crew. The lack of hassle probably helped to make the Three Creek Ranch a preferred destination for filming. Nobody needed more fuss in their life. She'd gotten enough fuss yesterday to last her all year. And she really didn't need to discover another mouse colony in her barn.

She waved a hand at Hector at the gate. The security guard and his clipboard were constant mainstays of any production, and he took his job very seriously. Not that the Three Creek Ranch Western Town and Backlot had ever experienced vandals or thieves. But thanks to the huge interest in *As The Heart Draws* there was intrigue about the set's location, and Hector had kept the odd fan or lost tourist away. It'd be nice if he steered his interest in her away too, but she'd learned the delicate art of suppressing hopes and killing off those rabbit trails of admiration in the effort to keep him on-side. His burly presence offered a feeling of protection she certainly didn't experience in the company of a certain actor who was supposed to be a hero. Harrison's presence instead held an unsettling quality, like he was dangerous.

She parked, shaking her head at her foolishness. Good thing

she wouldn't have to deal with him today. After retrieving Miranda, she opened the prop barn's door and entered the world of a bygone era.

The scent of age arose to meet her but, fortunately, she couldn't smell anything else. Miranda's reaction would soon make it plain if there was something to be concerned about. She opened the carrier's door, and sure as a bullet, Miranda streaked out, a silent blur of orange fur.

Cassie's heart tensed. But Miranda racing off like that didn't mean she'd spotted the enemy, more that she didn't like being cooped up in her travel cage.

Sure enough, after a thorough investigation of the premises, Miranda returned, her demeanor placid. The cat took to her chair, a plush vintage armchair one commandeered from a faith-friendly production from two years ago, and commenced licking herself, the sign that all was well.

"Thank You, God."

The next hours were spent fielding phone calls and counting stock for upcoming accountancy purposes, before a knock preceded the door opening.

"Hello?"

Cassie hurried down the aisle of framed sepia photographs to the front, where a young woman she hadn't seen before was peering around, her eyes huge. "Yes?"

The young woman startled, then smiled. "Are you Miss James?"

"Yep."

"Oh, hi. I'm Maxine. I'm the assistant to Mr. Woods."

Mr. Woods? Why didn't that name ring a bell? Was he one of the new crew or producers? "Okay. How can I help you?"

"I'm really sorry to interrupt you, but Mr. Woods has asked me to find alternative accommodation. I was told by Lance Fidler that there were some spare rooms in the town we could use."

"Yes." Cassie straightened, eyeing the young woman who

looked fresh out of college. "You weren't on set last year, were you?"

"No, I'm new."

Cassie nodded. "Okay. So, we do have a few rooms in the western town we've used for accommodation." She smiled. "Lincoln Cash stayed in one of them for a dare a few years ago."

Maxine grinned. "That must've been fun having him around."

"He was game for anything." Unlike a certain man who was scared of a mouse. She smirked. "Anyway, my dad and I spent last winter refurbishing some of those rooms for guest accommodation." As another revenue source for the ranch. "And while in the past we've had most of the cast and crew stay in trailers, some cast members"—like Tanner last year—"didn't like the claustrophobic feeling of them. So we thought we'd offer an alternative this year to the trailers, and if anyone wanted they could stay in one of our on-site apartments."

"Do they have bathrooms?" Maxine rolled her eyes. "Apparently that's a really important factor."

"They do."

"Good. And they're ready to go now?"

"Sure are." Cassie smiled. "I can put Mr. Woods in one of our nicest rooms at the back of the barber's. It's one of the biggest so he should feel quite comfortable there."

"Thank you." Maxine's nose wrinkled. "He gets a little fussy about some things, so if there's a chance to make things right I'd appreciate it."

"Fussy?" She didn't like to gossip, but none of the cast she knew could claim that characteristic. Apart from someone she'd deigned not to think about anymore.

The blonde grimaced. "Apparently there was a mouse in his trailer, and—"

Ah, bless. She might've known.

"—so that'd be awesome if you could help me out."

Cassie nodded. She'd be helping this poor woman out, even if she didn't really want to be helping out Harrison. His manner with her was too unnerving to ever be truly comfortable. She bet he still thought she was part of the crew. Which, to be fair, she kind of was. But still.

The reminder from her earlier prayer time drifted close again. *Fine, God.* She gritted her teeth and smiled. "I'll come with you now and show you where it is."

The barber's was situated in the middle of the town, but according to the production schedule notes was not destined to be used in filming in the booked time period. Of course, things could change, and a particular building be requested for use, which she'd happily oblige: hello, increased revenue. But the beauty of the apartments was that they were all tucked away at the back, in buildings on the perimeter. Each had separate entrances and were designed so that while filming happened in the front rooms, someone could be living in the back and nobody would be any wiser. She and her father had installed bathrooms that matched building codes but gave no hint of their modernity from the outside, drains and pipes all disguised by wooden piers and fascia.

She showed Maxine the room, which she approved, then for kicks showed her the front as well.

"Back in the day a barber's sometimes also operated as an undertakers and a morgue."

"A morgue?" Maxine glanced around like she expected a mummy to suddenly fall from a closet.

"Don't worry. We disposed of all the bodies we found. In the cemetery by the church."

Maxine's eyes rounded.

Cassie chuckled. "Just kidding. No dead bodies here, I promise."

Judging from Maxine's expression, Cassie wasn't sure she believed her. "But why would they do that?"

"I don't know. But in historical times, if there wasn't a dedicated undertaker, then I suppose the man you trusted with shaving your throat might also be entrusted with preserving bodies."

Maxine wrinkled her nose. "I don't think I'll tell him all that."

"Probably best not to."

After giving Maxine a key, Cassie opened the window to let in fresh air. And while part of her was sorely tempted to short-sheet Harrison's bed, another part—the part that was trying to listen to the Holy Spirit and follow in Jesus's footsteps—knew she had to let that antagonism die and show love instead.

Fine then. She'd make sure his apartment was the nicest it could possibly be. She might even deign to put fresh flowers in the room. And she'd be sure to put a Bible in a prominent position beside the bed, just like the Gideons used to do. Heaven knew the man needed it.

IT WAS late by the time he returned to his trailer, only to remember he'd been moved. But where? The day had been long, and he had a vague recollection of Maxine saying something, but where...?

He stabbed his phone and got her number. "Maxine? Where am I supposed to be?"

"Did you find the barber's?"

"The what?" He touched the back of his neck, then remembered what she had said earlier.

"The barber's in the western—"

"—town, I remember." He slapped his back pocket, found the key she'd handed to him several hours ago before exiting the site like most lowly production assistants did. Their accommodation wasn't supplied on-site, unlike those crew members with better pay grades. He frowned. So what did that make the cowgirl wannabe? She must be more important than he'd thought.

Shaking off thoughts of her—thank goodness she'd been

invisible today—he refocused on the matter at hand. "So, my stuff is all there?"

"Yep. You should be ready to move in."

"And there's definitely a real bathroom? I won't have to go trekking back to the backlot toilets in the middle of the night?" Probably TMI, but it was important. Growing up poor in a place that sometimes didn't have a functioning toilet left an impression on a man.

"You'll like it there, I promise. It's been renovated recently. I spoke to the owner and apparently Lincoln Cash stayed there before it got done up."

Huh. He didn't know whether to be more impressed by the fact his assistant had spoken to the owner when he still hadn't, or whether to be challenged by the fact that if Lincoln had stayed there, then he now had to as well. No way was he going to let that man outdo him any more than absolutely necessary.

"Thanks, then."

"Sleep well." She ended the call before he could say anything more.

Hmm. If he hadn't experienced a few more looks from Dana and the cook, he'd start to think he was losing his touch with women. And while he appreciated the fact that Maxine was new in this role, the fact a college girl came across as barely willing to give him the time of day felt weird, and more than a little wrong. That, combined with the cowgirl's indifference and antipathy... was he losing his charm?

He trekked back past the mess hall, waved to a few of the crew who were still up, then followed the solar flare-lit path up the hill. He paused on the crest. Here, the western town slept in moonlit glory, and his heart skipped a beat or two. If he didn't know better, he could've been transported back in time a century and a half. All it needed was for the saloon to have a few drunks whooping it up for a genuine 1800s vibe. But he was glad no drunks were here. He needed sleep, and the thought of fresh sheets and a real bed hurried him to where he thought the barber's might be.

But the town looked different in the night. He'd always prided himself on his sense of direction, but the streets appeared to have turned around from what he thought he knew. Even entering what he thought was the main street seemed different now.

He peered up at the overhangs, using his phone's flashlight to light the signs. Nope. That was the general store. That one, the haberdashers. A few steps further—nope. Harry's Saloon. Man. Where was the barber's?

The key was burning a hole in his back pocket, and he wondered at the wisdom of this. Maybe he should've stuck it out another night in the trailer. But two nights of interrupted sleep, knowing there was a mouse on the loose, was two nights too many. He'd flubbed his lines too many times today to feel comfortable about getting away with any more. Harrison could appreciate that Mal might be extending some grace to the newbie, but he suspected it'd pretty soon come across as unprofessional if it continued.

So where was the barber's?

He glanced at his phone, half tempted to call Maxine again. But surely that would just make him look even more lame than she already thought. He was a grown man, for goodness sake. It shouldn't be this hard.

A rustle from the hill raised the hairs on his neck. His fingers clenched. Nope. He didn't believe in ghosts, despite the fact there was a cemetery nearby. It was fake, right? But when the shivering sound was followed by a loud screech, his heartbeat increased, and he reached out a hand. Felt something move.

He shrieked, stumbling backwards, then falling over and into a water trough, and released another yell. "Are you freakin' kidding me?"

Sorely tempted to swear, he got up, his jeans now all wet, along with his smartwatch. He'd dropped his phone—hopefully not in the water—and checked the dirt, where he'd been standing. Took a step. Heard a crack. Did swear this time. He picked it up. Saw the cracked screen. Felt his heart fist. Whoever thought this was a good idea didn't have a clue about occupational health and safety. "This is ridiculous!"

Then a light flicked on in the chapel.

No way. Someone was there, all this time? Had they heard him scream? Oh, man, he hoped it wasn't—

He swallowed another word as a figure appeared. He recognized that white hat. What the heck was she doing out here at this time of night? Didn't she have a home to go to?

"Mr. Woods?" She held up her phone, its flashlight mode activated. In the reflected glow he could see her wide eyes as she scanned him, head to toe. "What on earth—?"

"Whoever is responsible for putting accommodation in this hick town should be shot!"

"Excuse me?"

"This place is filled with trip hazards! A person could die out here."

"A person could die anywhere, so I think you're being a little dramatic."

"I'm an actor. That's what we do. Especially when some fool leaves water in a trough and there's no light or guard rail to stop a person from falling into it."

She pressed her lips together, but the cough she gave sounded awfully like a smothered chuckle.

"It's not funny! I could've been seriously injured! I've got a good mind to sue whoever is responsible for this."

All amusement faded as she took a step forward. "Mr. Woods —"

Oh, he was Mr. Woods now, was he?

"—I'm very sorry this happened. We do have lights for nighttime, but I don't know why they weren't activated."

A faint bell rang at that last word, something else Maxine had said. But what?

"You're staying in the barber's, right?"

"Yes," he gritted out.

"Didn't Maxine give you instructions about turning on the power box at the top of the hill?"

He ground his teeth. Maybe she had.

"Have you had a chance to find your accommodation yet?"

"What do you think I've been trying to do for the last twenty minutes?"

"Oh, I'm so sorry. Truly, I am."

"Can you please just show me where I'm supposed to stay? I'm wet, tired, and really not in the mood to exchange small talk a second longer."

"Of course." Her voice was subdued. "Please come this way."

He followed her, and he wondered again at her role here. She seemed to be everywhere and have far greater involvement than what he'd first thought.

"Why were you at the chapel?"

She glanced at him. "Just finalizing a few more details for a wedding that's happening the weekend after this."

The weekend the production had off: a rare moment in an otherwise crammed schedule. He couldn't wait to get out of Dodge and maybe go visit Banff and experience some real accommodation, sleep in a real bed, enjoy some luxury and peace and quiet for a change. He had a feeling that whatever waited for him at the barber's wasn't going to be much better than that water trough.

"Just in here." She led down a small alley, then pointed to a door he hadn't noticed before. "Got your key?"

"Yeah."

He opened the back door, and she pointed to where the light switch was. He flicked it on, and instantly the room was bathed in soft light.

Huh. Far from being a decrepit spiderwebbed-dressed room a la Harry's Saloon, this place was almost as nice as the hotel suite he'd stayed in only a few nights ago.

The bed might not be king-sized, but it was big enough for him, and suited the space. He peeked inside the bathroom, surprised that the compact space held as much as it did, with a shower over bath, toilet and washbasin on what looked like a reclaimed dresser.

"I hope the hot water works," he muttered.

She flicked the faucet a few times, and a few seconds later steam rose from the bowl. "Looks like it does."

Okay, then.

She moved to the window, lowering it a little. "I wasn't sure if you'd prefer fresh air or not."

"I like fresh air but I don't want open windows if it means critters can get in."

"There's a screen." She smiled. "You'll be safe, I promise."

Hmph.

Here in the light he could see her better now, and after the past few days of staying away, he noticed she looked weary, dark smudges underscoring her eyes. "What are you doing working at this time of night?"

She shrugged. "Like I said, I had to sort some stuff for the wedding."

Why she was involved in the wedding when the production crew had that weekend off seemed weird to him. But who knew exactly what went on around here? Besides, he was too tired to care, and getting colder by the second.

"I'm sorry about the water trough," she said. "I do hope you won't hold it against us."

He sighed. "It's a hazard, that's what it is."

She nodded, her gaze falling to her boots, as if she was taking this personally.

"You just need to have those lights on," he added more gently.

"I'll make sure of it." She glanced up, but her face was expressionless, her gaze not touching his. "Was there anything else?"

"No. Thanks."

"I hope you have sweet dreams."

"I doubt it." Her lips pressed together again, and he realized how churlish that made him sound, so he quickly added, "I'm an actor. I have a vivid imagination. We'll see."

"Good night."

She shut the door with a gentle click, leaving him to survey the room and absorb the peace and ambiance. For all the room's updated features, he could also appreciate the ties to the past, such as the weathered wooden floorboards, and the cream-painted watering can that held an arrangement of sweet-smelling roses. Little touches that helped him get into feeling his character more. Little touches, like the oatmeal cookies in a glass jar beside the bed, with a handwritten note that said "Sweet dreams" that made him wonder if the cowgirl was responsible for that as well. Which was probably a step way too far for a mere production assistant, unless she really was someone who went the extra mile.

After showering in the best shower he'd had since home, he nibbled a cookie—surprisingly good—and checked through the small library of books in the armoire that also hid a TV. Louis L'Amour, Jack London, Larry McMurtry, Elmore Leonard, some girly looking stuff by someone called Janette Oke.

Next to his bed lay a Bible. He didn't dare touch it, but it lay there, taunting him.

Once upon a time he'd believed. Until the preacher's emphasis on God being a father had turned his stomach, as his own dad was no endorsement of anything good. Then life and busyness and fakery had gotten in the way. Distractions, his grandma would've called it.

He reached into his bag and pulled out the cameo, the talisman he often carried that he'd saved from one of his dad's drunken benders. His father had never valued anything of his grandmother's, but Harrison had known his mom would like it, even if it had resulted in the worst thrashing Harrison had received in his life.

Gladness filled him that his grandmother wasn't here to see the man he'd become, the shallow, petty man who complained about stupid things. She'd be ashamed of him. And because his Grandma had always been the gold standard by which he compared all women, she most likely would've been prodding him to change.

Easier said than done.

FIVE

Humiliation scorched Cassie's cheeks as she drove home. She who prided herself on doing things well had messed up. Harrison Woods might be an oaf of a man, but he was right. She should have ensured the lights were set to automatic sensor mode, but had gotten distracted in the myriad of tasks requiring her attention. And with the film crew here all day, the only time she had available to attend to the chapel was at night. Somehow, she'd forgotten that Harrison would be using the room and might appreciate being able to see. And while it had been funny to see what had happened to him, all amusement fled when she realized just how dangerous the situation could have been.

By the time she got home, her stomach was churning at her mistake.

Her sister recognized her pressure when she walked through the door. "Cass?"

She sighed, slumping onto the sofa in front of the TV where a movie was paused.

"What are you doing home so late?" Jess asked.

"I needed to double check the chapel."

"For the wedding?"

"Mm-hm. I had to measure some things, and make sure it was all fine."

"And is it?"

"It will be." *Please God, let it all go smoothly.*

"They're not using it for the filming?"

"They've agreed to wait until after the wedding, so that's something."

Jess eyed her. "Are you doing okay? You look a little stressed."

"I'm fine."

Jess smirked. "Yeah, sorry sis, but that's not the face of fine."

"Rude." She found a smile.

Jess had no corresponding one. "It's honest, which is more than what I think you're being. Come on, Cassie. I don't understand how you keep up with all you are doing. Helping dad with running the ranch—"

Yeah, she'd hardly be helping with that lately.

"—and all this stuff with the show and the western town, and now organizing a wedding. You're taking on too much."

"I'm coping." Barely.

Jess folded her arms. "I don't think you really are. Can you get some helpers with the western town?"

"I could if I could afford to pay them."

Jess winced. "It's not making money yet?"

"It's seasonal, and with the money we outlaid for the new bathrooms and upgraded accommodation last winter, I've been counting on the *As The Heart Draws* payments to cover that." That, and the fee from the movie that had been cancelled. "It's a juggle, but we'll get there." Cassie shrugged. "And in the meantime, I'll keep working my long hours until we can justify paying someone else to help with it."

"I just worry—and I've heard Mom say this too—that you're working too hard. You need a chance to have a break."

Good thing Mom and Dad weren't here to hear this conversation. They likely were asleep already. Her parents had long believed in early to bed, early to rise, with the associated benefits of health, wealth and wisdom. She didn't like to think she was concerning her mom. But saying that aloud would only make it seem more real, so she concentrated on the other part of her sister's sentence. "A break would be nice, and once the wedding is over, I'm sure we'll get one."

"Hmm."

Cassie didn't have time for her sister's doubt-laden hmm-ing. "I should go have a shower. I feel like I've lived three days today."

"I feel like this conversation isn't done yet."

"Too bad." She smirked at Jess.

"Hey, got any more word about this Saturday?"

This Saturday? What was—? Oh. A groan escaped. "Man, I keep forgetting I'm supposed to organize Hannah's bachelorette party, and I haven't yet."

"What can I help with?" Jess asked.

"Everything?"

Jess raised her eyebrows.

"I mean it. All I've asked is for people to save the date and given them a start time, but I haven't booked anything yet. And okay, you may be right and I'm spinning too many plates in life. I don't know why I said yes to this. I feel like I'm walking through quicksand and life is about to suck me down."

"Cassie."

Her sister's look of compassion drew her throat tight. See, this was why she liked to play pretend as much as any actor. Accidental truth bombs where she admitted she couldn't do it all only left her feeling emotional and exposed, like she wasn't good enough, would never be enough. And yeah, maybe over the years she'd shouldered more than her fair share of responsibility to help others live their dreams. They'd all had to sacrifice in various ways when Franklin chased his NHL ambitions, and again when Jess and Poppy pursued their respective goals of veterinary and professional dancing careers. Cassie's heart had always been for the ranch, but even though she knew ranch-life wasn't glamorous, it didn't stop her sometimes feeling less-than, and like she had to work triply hard to prove herself. She swallowed a boulder-sized lump. Except when it ended up proving that she couldn't.

Jess straightened in her seat. "How many people are we talking?"

"Eight? Ten? Hannah doesn't have any family—apart from her mom, and Hannah was pretty clear that she didn't want her there—so Bree Vaughan, some friends from work and church. And us."

"Did she say what she wanted to do?"

"Nothing too cheesy, or expensive. But just because it's not expensive doesn't mean we can do cheap."

Jess nodded. "Sounds like we should ask Poppy, the party queen, to give us some advice."

Poppy was staying in Franklin's apartment in the city, as she and Jess sometimes did while he was away. It made it easier for them to get to work and participate in the social life Poppy enjoyed. Poppy was notorious for late nights, so there was no harm in seeing if she was available to talk now. "Go for it."

A minute later, Poppy was on FaceTime, and they were tossing around suggestions. Weight was slipping from Cassie's shoulders as they firmed up a plan. A swim in the creek—warranted by the weekend's expected heat, and a nice reminder of how Hannah and Franklin had first met—followed by high tea and movies, all of which would guarantee an easy, chilled vibe. It wouldn't cost too much, would be something relaxing that Hannah would like, and would show off the ranch.

"That sounds so good." Cassie sighed. "Thanks guys."

"Hey, three heads are better than one," Jess said.

"That's for sure." Gosh, she loved her sisters. "I really appreciate your help with this."

"You've had a lot on your plate lately," Jess reminded her.

"You're doing too much," Poppy said, direct as always.

"But I'm Hannah's best friend and maid of honor, so I should be taking care of this."

"You know Franklin said he was happy to pay for a wedding coordinator," Poppy reminded her.

"But it wouldn't have been as personal," Cassie objected.

"It wouldn't have stressed you out as much," Jess said.

True. "I just didn't expect the start of this season to be so much busier than the last."

Jess's brows rose. "So what's different this year?"

A certain somebody who didn't like mice, for starters.

"What's that look for?" Poppy asked. "Is there an actor who's hit on you?"

"Ha! Try just the opposite."

"Deets, please."

"No, nothing like that." She still couldn't admit to the identity of the show's new leading man. "Let's just say that God is reminding me that I'm supposed to be gracious."

"Ooh, intriguing!"

No, it wasn't. It was disturbing how much that man had the power to disconcert her. She'd dealt with other guys who'd hit on her effectively, dampening pretensions with a well-executed arch of eyebrow or well-timed remark, or when God had reminded her to turn the other cheek. And while she didn't expect Harrison Woods to ever hit on her, she didn't like feeling she was someone he wanted to avoid. They might have agreed to avoid each other, but that now felt stupidly petty. And the fact she was still thinking about this proved she'd given him entirely too much power in her mind.

"Hey, do you have that accommodation thing happening yet?" Poppy asked.

She nodded. "That's part of it." She explained about the trailer and the mouse, and the last-minute change of accommodation, internally high-fiving herself at not naming names.

"What kind of man is scared of a mouse?" Jess asked. "At least he didn't kill it."

"I hope your props are okay," Poppy said.

"Me too. I took Miranda today and she seemed to think it was all good."

"You need a break."

She sure did. But even with the promise of an afternoon off this Saturday to celebrate Hannah's soon-to-end single status, the wedding itself loomed just the weekend after. Maybe after that she could finally relax.

THE BEST NIGHT's sleep of his life had been followed by three days of filming where he'd been so busy it was all he could do to eat his meal with the cast at night before he tumbled into bed. But finally, it felt like he was fitting in. He was remembering names, and more importantly, remembering his lines, and he got the impression that Mal didn't think employing Harrison was such a mistake anymore. The scenes he'd been shooting had involved everything from time with his Mountie colleagues to scenes shot with Ainsley where they first met.

He liked when a production schedule allowed for a more natural chemistry to develop between people. He'd shot some movies where the shooting schedule meant he'd had to film a scene and grieve a character he hadn't actually met yet. Here, where the actors all knew each other and had spent time together, really made it feel like a family. And the fact he didn't have much of a family himself—his grandmother had basically raised him, after his parents proved they couldn't—meant he was starting to relax into the rhythms of this cast.

And now, they were eating lunch on Friday, the weekend beckoned, and he felt like he had a chance to breathe.

"This is good, huh?" He motioned to the salad the caterers provided.

Ainsley smiled. "I don't mind admitting I ask them to make chicken Caesar salad every Friday. It gives me the boost to finish the week well."

"I think people underestimate how much food can make or break a production."

"Right? And when it's healthy but still tastes nice, it's even better."

"Amen." Part of the double standard of filming: women were far more likely to hear murmurs of needing to "watch your calorie intake" than a man, with everything from costume fittings to proposed methods of transport potentially affected by an additional few pounds. A man had it easier, with none of the waist-cinching corsets and clothes that were deemed historically accurate, when an hourglass figure was a legit goal. Moments like that made him extra thankful to be a man.

Ainsley's head had tilted, and she was studying him, a small smile on her dial.

"What is it?" he asked.

"I was just wondering, do you mean that?"

"Mean what?"

"Amen."

He shrugged. "It's what you say when you agree with someone."

"I know. But I just wondered if it meant you were a…"

"A what?"

Her voice lowered. "A believer."

"A believer?"

Her face shadowed. "I guess that's my answer."

"You mean a Christian?"

She nodded, her look hopeful once again.

He was about to answer, and probably dial that look of hers back to nothing, when Jerry, one of the lead writers, interrupted with an apology and stole Ainsley's attention.

He looked back over his lines, committing them to memory, imagining the scene as it would play out.

Ainsley's smile and patience with the crew continued as that conversation was immediately followed by one with Glenda, the chief costume fitter, who wanted to check with her about something else. Man, Ainsley sure was patient. He'd noticed it on display each day she'd been on set.

"Sorry about that," Ainsley said, when Glenda had gone.

He studied her. "Why are you so nice all the time?"

"Nice?" Ainsley's brows knit, like she wasn't sure whether he'd meant that as a compliment or a sneer.

"It's a compliment, Ainsley. You're so patient. Like, all the time. How do you do it?"

Her mouth pulled to one side. "Well, I certainly don't feel patient all the time. There are some things I've been waiting on for what feels like forever." She tucked her long dark hair behind her ear. "But I've learned that people don't need my impatience or my attitude when things don't go my way. We need more kindness in this world, don't you think?"

"Yeah."

"I think patience is a byproduct of kindness, which stems from love, and realizing that we all can do with more love."

Was that an invitation to find out if she meant she wanted a relationship? "Am I hearing you say you want someone to love you?"

"No." Her cheeks pinked, as she looked directly at him. "I know I'm loved. And I'm not talking about needing a man to love, but knowing we are all loved by God. That's what ultimately motivates me in how I treat others."

Huh. So Ainsley Beckett was a Christian, and one of those rare ones who actually tried to live out what they believed.

But he didn't need that. He needed distraction, but not by believing in invisible people. Maybe once upon a time he'd thought the whole God thing was true, but he'd soon learned it wasn't.

And he was relieved when a production assistant called out that it was time to resume.

. . .

Saturday's filming schedule saw him released at lunch. Ainsley had new scenes to shoot, but he'd gotten the afternoon off. And while part of him was tempted to drive into the city and steal a few hours of sanity in the real world, the fact that he didn't really have friends around here made him hesitate. Truth be told, Ainsley and Dustin were about the only cast members he'd consider friends. Dana was more like one to avoid, and he'd already turned down her invitation to dinner at Steak and Majors, Calgary's premium steakhouse, fearing it would only fuel gossip about him he really didn't need.

But staying on-site made him itchy. And given today's heat, he didn't want to stay inside. Perhaps he could practice his riding by using one of the horses.

Thirty minutes later, he was astride a horse named Buddy, one of the horses owned by a nearby ranch. The horse wrangler, Ted, was mounted on his own horse, Nancy, and was giving him tips as he rode around the corral.

"You're doing nicely," Ted called. "Try not to move up and down too much, even it out a little."

Harrison tried to follow the instructions, but his legs were getting sore. Not that he'd admit that. No way did he want a reputation for complaining any more than he already did. He grasped the horse's sides with his knees, and Buddy slowed.

"Man."

"I don't know about you, but I think Buddy might be getting a little bored in here. Want to hit some trails?"

"You mean we can go further afield?"

Ted nodded. "One of the reasons we love this place so much is that the ranch owners basically give us license to use the surrounding acres. And we're talking thousands of acres."

"Imagine being that rich."

Ted shrugged. "I like that it's a family business, and the Three Creek Ranch has been in the same family for generations. It's not one of these corporations that buy up ranches like what often happens these days."

Yeah, he supposed that was a good thing. "So, where do you want to go?"

"There's a stream not too far away. I bet Buddy would like the chance to stretch his legs, and it'll give you somewhere new to see."

"We can just go there?"

"As long as if we open any gates we close them behind us, then the owners are happy for us to use the land. It's not like the cattle aren't used to people on horseback, either. And I think the James family don't mind us keeping an eye on things to make sure their stock is safe too. Come on. It'll be fun. More fun than baking to a crisp hanging around here in the sun."

"Sounds good."

A short time later he was cantering across the long grass, beyond the western town. Judging from the tree shadows this direction was north. He wondered how long it would take to ride to the main road, then wondered about who maintained all this land. It was one thing to have thousands of acres, but it must take a huge team to mend fences and keep livestock safe.

But he could appreciate why they hadn't sold their land. The vistas here were amazing, the view to the Rockies like a cowboy's dream. He reined in Buddy and drank it in, before a faint sound drew his attention. He glanced to the side, cocking his ear.

Ted turned Nancy back and drew alongside. "All good?"

"I thought I heard something."

Ted grinned. "That'd be the sound of enjoyment. Go on, you can tell me. You're enjoying riding, aren't you?"

"It's not as bad as I remember."

"I'm counting that as a win."

"And I do appreciate the trouble you're taking with me."

"Oh, yeah, it's a real hardship going for a ride in this beautiful area. Such a chore." Ted pulled out his phone, read a message, winced. "I gotta go. One of the horses is sick. Now you remember which way we came?"

"That way?" He pointed in the direction he thought they came.

"Good. I'll see you there soon. Take it easy and you'll be fine, okay?"

Ted took off, not waiting for an answer, but something held Harrison back. He didn't want to speed home—Ted was clearly in a hurry, and Harrison would only slow him down—and he was still curious about the sound he'd heard before. It had sounded like a shout, like someone was hurt, and if that was the case, then he couldn't leave whoever it was here. Memories flashed of his mom, her cries of pain, while he'd hidden under the bed.

He shook his head, trying to free himself of the memories. It wouldn't be that bad, surely. Although, while Ted had assured that there weren't bears around here, how could the man be sure? This ranch was huge, and what exactly was stopping a bear, or bear posse, from moving down from the mountains to get themselves a nice meal of prime beef? He'd seen the cattle around here. They were huge, and looked like just the right sort of animal to tempt a hungry bear to a snack. And it wouldn't take much longer for the bear to find the injured human and be persuaded to snack on them instead. So it was only right that he check on the source of the sound and make sure all was okay.

He stayed still, waiting. Then the cry came again. There! From the right.

"Come on, Bud." He patted the horse's neck. "Let's go find out who's in trouble."

His heart beat faster as he steered Buddy down the hill, near the rocks where he was fairly sure the sound had originated. After all his recent misses, this was his chance to be a hero. It was just a shame that certain people—okay, a certain cowgirl—wouldn't be around to witness it. But that was okay. Ted might find it in his heart to subtly tell people how Harrison had saved the day, and he'd just need to look humble. And he could do humble. He could do humble very well, thank you very much.

He smirked as Buddy trotted around a large rock, situated on what looked like an embankment. In fact, he could act like the humblest person ever in the history of the world, and—

"Whoa!"

He pulled Buddy to a stop, and stared at the scene below.

Below, where in a small river, several swimsuit-clad women were lying on large floating mattresses—was that a pink flamingo? —and obviously not in any trouble at all.

But he sure would be, as soon as any of them looked up here and noticed him, and said—

"Hey!"

He glanced across, and his jaw dropped. No way.

Cowgirl Cassie might not be wearing her white hat, but he'd recognize that look of contempt anywhere. Although, he swallowed, he hadn't exactly expected *that* figure under the jeans and long-sleeve shirt.

She crossed her arms, and he hefted his gaze up to meet her eyes. Her stormy eyes. "What are you doing?"

"Whoa! I didn't think you'd arrange a stripper, Cassie!" one of the women called.

A what?

"Oh my gosh," Cassie mumbled, before shouting, "I didn't, and he's leaving!" She turned to him. "Go away."

"Gladly." He didn't know what was going on but he had no wish for more of the cowgirl's disdain. He wasn't feeling that brave.

"No, don't make him go," the voice from earlier said. "It was just getting interesting."

"Hurry up," Cassie growled at him.

"Come on, Bud." He nudged his horse.

"Aww, handsome guy, don't run away," the woman from below pleaded.

He peered at them, then raised his hand. "Sorry ladies, I'm gonna have to love you and leave you."

"You don't have to!"

"Yes, you do," Cassie said. "Go."

He glanced back at her, that earlier moment of wishing to flee departing. "What happens if I don't?"

Her eyes narrowed. "You know you're trespassing."

"Am I? I was told this was land that was available to be used by all the cast and crew."

"Who told you that?"

"Ted."

"Hmph. Well, this side is." She then pointed to the creek. "That side isn't."

"So, excuse me for being dumb, but why are you and your friends on that side?"

Her eyes narrowed further, but before she could answer, another of the bikini-clad women drew alongside her. This one looked younger, obviously not body conscious, unlike Cassie who still looked like she wanted to wrap herself in an invisibility cloak and disappear.

She shaded her eyes as she glanced from Cassie up to himself, still in the saddle. "Who are you?"

"Harrison. And you?"

"Poppy." She glanced at Cassie again. "You two know each other?"

"Hardly."

"What she means to say is that 'she would like to know me more, but is afraid of the sheer amount of animal magnetism I possess'," he said, quoting one of his lines from an obscure indie movie he'd done several years ago.

"The sheer amount of something you possess," Cassie muttered.

Poppy laughed, then her eyes widened. "Wait. You're not that actor, are you?"

"It depends."

Cassie sighed. "Don't encourage him, Poppy. He needs to go."

"And you're here because you're one of the actors on set, aren't you?" Poppy gasped. "Does this mean you've taken Tanner's role on *As The Heart Draws*?"

"Ah…" How was he supposed to explain that?

"Oh no!"

Okay. Not the reaction he'd expected.

Cassie sighed. "Poppy, can you please leave the man alone? He needs to go." She stepped closer and hissed up at him, "See? You need to scram. You're making things difficult."

"No! He needs to stay." Poppy's chin tilted. "I have questions."

"Save them for another day." Cassie looked up at him. "Please leave. This is awkward enough already, and you staying is just making things worse."

"But nobody is embarrassed except you," Poppy said, before gesturing to where the half dozen other women were watching them. All they needed was popcorn. "Look, even Hannah is cool."

But it was clear that Cassie wasn't. Her lips compressed more tightly, even as Poppy called out "Hannah!" which elicited a wave from one of the women below.

He peered at her. Something about her face was familiar. "Wait—is that the sports reporter?"

"Hannah Wade." Poppy slung an arm around Cassie's shoulder. "Soon to be our sister-in-law."

"Our?" He glanced back at Cassie. She ducked her head, her shoulders slumping. "No way. Is Franklin James—the hockey player for the Flames—is he your brother?"

"The one and the same," a third woman, a brunette, joined them. "I'm Jess."

"Harrison," he said automatically, recognizing the similar features shared by the three women.

Jess peered at her sister then back at him. "Aha."

Uh oh. That kind of look never boded well. "What has she said?"

"Nothing," Cassie snapped, at the same time Jess said, "Nothing."

"Ooh, but there's definitely something." Poppy smirked at Jess. "Wouldn't you agree?"

"One hundred percent."

Cassie huffed out a breath. "Fine. Stay. Go. I don't care what you do. But you should probably get Buddy out of the sun. It's too hot and he'll need a drink."

"He could have a drink here." He nudged Buddy to move forward.

"It's too steep," Cassie warned. "You need to be careful."

Then, as if her words had lit a match, Buddy lowered his head to drink from the creek, and Harrison's inattention triggered his clumsy genes again, and he tumbled off and landed in the creek with a splash.

Six

S*plash!*

Cassie froze, hands covering her mouth, her shoulders relaxing as Harrison stumbled upright, exclaiming about the icy cold water. Thank goodness the man hadn't done himself a real injury.

"Oh my gosh. Are you okay?"

He peered at her, then shook his hair like a dog.

Water flicked and flew and landed on her. "Classy."

He smirked. "You know it."

"Are you sure you're okay?" Jess asked him, brow pleated. "I'm a vet, not a doctor, but I've had some medical training..."

"I'm fine. Clumsy, but fine."

"Well, if that's the case, then feel free to leave." Cassie crossed her arms again. The nerve of the man, scaring her like that. If he wanted to sue her for tripping over a water trough, imagine what he'd do breaking his spine while performing acrobatics on—or off—a horse.

"Cass! You can't make him leave," protested Poppy.

"Apparently," Cassie grouched.

He chuckled, and she glanced quickly at him. Now he was standing on land he wasn't that much taller. Half a head, if that, so not nearly as tall as Franklin. He did have nice eyes, and maybe even a sense of humor, seeing he'd laughed at her comment.

But it didn't mean she liked him. And it definitely didn't mean that she was comfortable with all of Hannah's friends glancing at her then at him then smiling, like this was a set up she'd somehow arranged. Which she had *not*.

"Come on, Cassie. Don't make me leave," he pleaded.

She crossed her arms then lifted them slightly, hiding any hint of cleavage. It wasn't that her one-piece was too revealing, but there was a world of difference between feeling comfortable while wearing a swimsuit with her friends, and standing in front of a handsome man who made her nervous. And it definitely didn't help to know her sister's dance-honed physique would forever appear to advantage, especially in comparison to Cassie's own, complete with farmer's tan.

"Besides," Harrison continued. "You haven't answered my question."

"Which one was that?"

"Why you're here and not over there. I mean, I get that your brother is famous, and Hannah probably even more so, but you only work at the movie set, right?"

Wow. How the man had ever managed to convincingly play a law professor she had no idea. Maybe he was a good actor, after all.

"You're kidding right?" Jess said, her arms folded, her face now holding a frown. "Cassie is one of the hardest working women around."

Thanks, Jess.

Jess glanced at her. "Does this man honestly not know who you are?"

"It doesn't matter," she murmured.

"Cassie *James*. Does that ring a bell?"

"Jess," she murmured.

"James?" He glanced at her. "That's your last name?"

"Oh my gosh," Jess muttered. "That's why she's Cassie James." She rolled her eyes.

"Where have I heard that name recently?"

One second, two seconds, three…

His eyes widened. "Your family owns this ranch?"

Cassie dipped her chin.

"Whoa." He staggered back, like her nod had held volcanic power.

Yeah, that's right, mister. She bit back a smile. "So really, my friends and I can go swimming anyplace we like. So if it's all the same to you, I'm going to go do that and you're gonna leave and we're all gonna be happy. Even Poppy." She wrapped an arm around her sister and tugged her away. "Even Poppy will be happy, because none of us want to hold you up from all the important things that you should be doing."

"Wait." Poppy scrambled away. "I'm not happy. I'd actually be a lot happier if I could find out exactly why you are trying to keep us away from him."

"Fine." Her sister was stubborn, and already this encounter had stolen far too much time and emotional energy. "You do you. I don't care, but I do care that this is Hannah's special day and right now none of us are talking to her, and I'm not okay with that. So, goodbye," she said to Harrison. Then she turned and waded across to the other side of the creek where the rest of the women waited. The women whose wide eyes and smiles said they were enjoying the show.

"Spill. Now." Bree Vaughan pointed to Cassie. "All the details. Go."

She sighed. The wife of Calgary's hockey captain was super sweet, but saw romance wherever she went. And this was definitely not what she'd planned for today. "There are no details. He's working nearby and came by accidentally." She hoped.

"Working?" Hannah, ever the reporter, asked. "He doesn't look like a cowboy."

"He's an actor," she mumbled.

"On *As The Heart Draws*?" Bree asked.

She couldn't very well lie now, could she? "Yes."

Bree's purply-gray eyes widened. "He's not the new love interest, is he? Oh my gosh. Does that mean Tanner is dead?"

Why, oh why had she ever told her friends that *As The Heart Draws* was filming here? "You know I can't reveal that."

"That sounds like a yes to me." Bree turned to Hannah. "Does that sound like a yes to you?"

"It does indeed."

"Guys, please don't ask," Cassie begged. "He's here and that's all I've got to say about that."

"*Is* that all?" Hannah prodded, with a teasing smile.

"That is all."

"I suspect that's not all." Hannah grinned. "But I'm having too much fun watching you pretend there isn't, that I don't care if it's an accident that he's here. I'm glad that our Cassie is not made of stone."

"Amen." Bree lifted her plastic glass of virgin margarita, one of the little Poppy touches that had elevated the creek swim into something more resembling a tropical getaway. That, and various other things, like the blow-up pink flamingo.

"I'm not made of stone," Cassie grumbled. "It's just he's annoying."

"Aw, don't be hard on the man," Bree protested. "It was an accident he arrived here, you said."

"No, I mean he's been really annoying for a while now. And I've got enough going on that I don't need to have more drama in my life."

"Drama." Bree winked at Cassie. "I see what you did there."

Cassie pasted a smile on her face and stood. "Anybody need a drink?"

She refilled glasses, then picked up a pink air mattress and dragged it further upstream to the bend in the creek where the tiny rapids bubbled and played. She needed to get away, to relax again, to not have this moment that she'd been enjoying spoiled by the man who apparently thought himself entitled to crash any event anywhere simply because he had a nice smile. Probably a bleached smile, she thought grumpily. But at least he hadn't chipped a tooth in his tumble. The ranch sure couldn't afford an actor's dental bills.

"Hey, Cassie, wait up."

She paused as Hannah dragged the flamingo behind her. "I thought you wanted to sun bathe."

"I did, and I have. And now I'm ready for another swim, if that's okay."

"Of course it's okay. You're the bride-to-be, so whatever you say goes."

"Hey."

Hannah's voice stayed Cassie's feet.

"I'm sorry for teasing you."

"It's okay."

"Clearly it's not." Hannah's bottom lip tucked in.

"It's just a lot. And I know I probably deserve it, but it's been a big week, and I'm tired, and now to feel like I'm the butt of everyone's jokes, I need some time away." Especially from him.

"Ah. It's hard to feel like you're under scrutiny, isn't it?"

And nobody would know that better than Hannah, whose high-profile sports reporter job on TV, combined with a high-profile boyfriend-now-fiancé, meant there were always people watching her, judging her. Hannah had been subjected to some horrendous online abuse from people protesting the fact a woman might dare to report on men's sports. Knowing her friend had received death threats made this afternoon's episode feel like a giant overreaction.

Cassie sighed. "I'm such a child sometimes."

"No, you're just tired. And it's hard when you're tired to let some of the silly little things slide." Hannah ghosted a smile. "Ask me how I know."

Cassie's heart panged. Today wasn't supposed to be about pain from the past, but was supposed to be about celebrating all things Hannah. She forced down her self-focused thoughts, and smiled at her friend. "Are you all set for next weekend? No silly little things bothering you?"

"No. It's all good. ESPN gave me Friday off, so that's taken off some pressure too."

"Then the wedding, then two weeks away somewhere tropical."

"Is that where he's taking me?"

Big internal wince. Between the accidental truth spill about Harrison's role on the show and now this, obviously she couldn't be trusted with any secret. "I can neither confirm nor deny."

"I don't care where we go. Two weeks of sleep and food and rest sounds like heaven to me."

"I don't think that's all you're supposed to do on a honeymoon." Cassie winked.

Hannah blushed. "Come on. Last one back to the others is a rotten you-know-what."

Cassie chased her to the water's edge and flung herself onto the air mattress, allowing the creek's gentle movements to guide her as she grasped the front edge. But unlike Hannah, whose competitive nature was always determined to win, she was content to avoid the others—and Harrison, if he dared to remain —a little longer.

She still couldn't explain why he pressed her buttons so much. Couldn't explain why she found his arrogance so frustrating. He should be nothing to her. He *was* nothing to her. Just a person she'd had the misfortune to meet. But there remained this weird connection, like an invisible string between them, that tugged and pulled and made her aware of him when she really didn't want to be.

"Lord, is it wrong to dislike someone so intensely?"

Her whisper got lost among the ripples and insect hum. Which was probably just as well as it was one of those dumb prayers that she already knew the answer to.

"Okay, God. I know that was a stupid thing to ask. But I

don't like feeling this way. And I need Your help to change my heart because I'm not shining much of Jesus right now, am I?"

Her eyes pricked, and she dragged her fingers through the water, not wanting to hear God's *Amen*. But changing her heart had to involve more than just words, more than a mouthed prayer. Experience had taught her that to change her attitude towards someone involved praying a blessing upon them. Each time she prayed a blessing it was like God chipped away at the stone walls around her heart, until one day her heart was soft. Witness what had happened with the twists and turns of her friendship with Hannah. They'd been friends in school, then Hannah had met Franklin right here in this very creek when she'd been sixteen, and everyone could see the sparks that had flown. But then Franklin had moved to Boston, and she and Hannah had drifted apart, and part of Cassie had resented her friend for leaving her. She hadn't known Hannah was facing her own battles with family dramas like her dad leaving, but it had hurt at the time. Until God had reminded her to pray for her friend, which she had, so when Hannah had returned to their lives last year Cassie could warmly welcome her in with a hug that held not a drop of acrimony.

Of course, she had no intention of welcoming Harrison into her family, nor hugging him *ever*, but it couldn't hurt to pray for the man, and not treat him as a nuisance. Even if he was.

"Sorry God." Clearly this being kind to Harrison thing was going to take some getting used to.

By the time her air mattress had gently bumped down to where the others waited, she was almost reconciled within her heart. She was grateful for this time to relax, and would try to let the rest of the day gently lead her, just as the water had done. Life was too short to get upset about everything.

"Hey Cassie!" someone called.

She peeked across at the shore. Her heart dipped. Looked like Harrison had continued to ignore her wish for him to leave, sitting there with his jeans rolled up to his knees, laughing like he didn't have a care in the world. Still, "God bless him," she gritted out.

"Cassie!" Jess shouted.

"What?" She staggered upright and checked to ensure that her float time lying on her front meant her swimsuit was still covering all the essentials. Phew. She boosted her air mattress under her arm.

"Don't move!" Harrison yelled.

Huh? Why was he running at her, like he wasn't going to stop?

Then he paused, and picked her up, just as a blur of brown and orange stripes leapt from the water and struck.

Harrison groaned, but kept carrying Cassie away from the snake.

"What are you doing?" she yelled, squirming. "Put me down!"

"Can't," he panted, clambering to the shore. Who knew where it was?

"Keep still," Jess commanded, authority in her voice.

He didn't know if she was speaking to him or her sister, but figured it was wisest to obey. As a vet, she should know how to deal with snakes.

Snakes? He shuddered, then peeked down at his leg. From just below his rolled-up jeans the snake had attached itself to his calf. He almost dropped Cassie.

His pulse drummed loudly in his ears, drowning out the shrieks from the other women. But above his intense fear, was awareness of this woman in his arms, how huge her blue-green eyes were, how close her face was to his, how easy it would be to bend his head and lower his mouth and—

"What are you doing?" Cassie demanded, flinching, shifting away.

"Cassie, keep still," Jess snapped. "He's been bitten by a snake because he was trying to protect you."

"A snake?" Cassie whispered, shrinking into his arms.

He clutched her more tightly. Maybe those heart-hammering nerves were more to do with this woman he held...

"Steady. Gosh, you're a big boy, aren't you?"

Excuse me? Oh, Jess was talking to the snake.

Jess gently divested his calf from the snake's mouth, and moved away to release it.

"Oh my gosh! He's bleeding!" one of the women called. Poppy? He couldn't remember much of anything anymore.

Wooziness clutched him, and he staggered.

"Whoa." Jess had returned. "You can put her down now. We need to deal with your wound."

Cassie wriggled, and he realized afresh that a woman wearing a swimsuit wriggling in his arms was a pretty effective distraction from a snake bite.

He lowered her, and she nearly jumped from his arms, straight into the beach towel held out by one of her friends, wrapping herself in it most securely, before glancing at him with wide eyes.

Hmm. Was that concern for him or concern at what he'd done? Her wince made him glance down again at his leg, where blood was freely flowing.

Jess tugged his arm. "You should sit down. I need to bind this up."

"What if there are other snakes here?" one of the other women asked.

"I hate snakes," another one whined. "They should all be killed."

Amen.

"You can't do that," Cassie said. "They're not out to get you. Snakes have an important role to play in the environment by killing pests and rodents. They're just trying to do their thing."

Huh.

"In over twenty years of coming here I've never seen a snake until today," Poppy said.

Jess ripped the flimsy pink fabric of what looked to be a sarong and padded one strip on the puncture mark, then wrapped the other section around his calf. "And I'm sure this one is non-venomous."

"How sure are you?" he asked.

"Pretty sure."

He'd rather one hundred percent certainty, but okay.

"There's so much blood," one of the other women murmured.

"I want to get out of here," another said.

"Ignore them." Cassie moved in front of them, drawing his attention. Her smile, tentative, but definitely friendlier than nearly every other encounter, ensured his gaze remained there.

Even with a towel around her and with wet hair clumping around her shoulders she was attractive. Her blue eyes held a slight hint of green, her dark lashes making the color pop against her tan. And now, when she wasn't busy being angry or offended at him, her face held a softness that made him want to try harder to be the kind of man his grandma would've been proud of, rather than the one his father had once called a slick faker.

"There." Jess tightened a bandage.

"Ow."

She glanced up at him then stood. "Now just because it's non-venomous doesn't mean it won't hurt. This type of garter snake has mildly venomous saliva, and may result in some pain and swelling, but less than you might usually expect in a snakebite."

"I gotta admit I don't usually expect a snake to bite me." Look at him, toughing it out, making jokes, being brave.

"You may end up with some swelling," Jess continued. "And you need to keep an eye out in case there is an allergic reaction. You should count yourself lucky it didn't do what it often does when threatened and release a stink bomb of a secretion."

"Hallelujah," he muttered. Still, he was grateful for small mercies.

Jess frowned. "We should send you to a doctor."

"There's a medic on set." Although how he was going to get there remained to be seen.

"I'll drive you back." Poppy gestured to the bank above. "My car is up there."

"You don't have to."

Jess wrinkled her nose. "Yeah, you're not going back on a horse."

"Cassie or Jess can ride Buddy," Poppy said.

A sigh escaped the woman he'd tried to save. He glanced at her apologetically. "I didn't mean to cause so much trouble."

"Says the man who refused to leave before."

Hmm. Clearly his heroics hadn't dampened all antagonism.

"We should get you back to civilization as soon as possible," one of the other women said, collecting their things. "Do you need ibuprofen?"

"No, don't take it," Jess cautioned. "His blood may be thinned, and it's already not clotting like it should." She frowned at him. "Do you have platelet issues?"

"What issues?"

"Your blood platelets. You know, the cells that allow for your blood to clot when you cut yourself."

"I don't think so."

"We'd better get you seen by a hospital doctor to make sure."

Great. How had a simple afternoon's ride turned into such a debacle? He glanced at the bride-to-be. "I'm really sorry for wrecking your afternoon."

"It's not wrecked. Just a little more dramatic than we expected."

"Drama is what he does," Cassie muttered, her gaze meeting his for a second before sliding away.

So much for making amends.

But there was no time to apologize again, as he was hustled to

Poppy's vehicle and gently pushed inside, while the other women stowed various pieces of paraphernalia in other cars.

And as Poppy reversed, he caught sight of Cassie, wading across the creek again and collecting his horse, her slumped shoulders saying this was not how she'd planned her day.

It certainly wasn't how he'd planned his, either.

SEVEN

"Thanks, Ted. I really appreciate it." Cassie ended the call, gave Buddy one last nose rub, then moved to her pickup where Hannah sat waiting. The others had loaded the other vehicles while Cassie had secured the horse in a small corral not far from the creek. What a train wreck of an afternoon this had been. "Ted said he'd come get Buddy soon."

"Will he be okay by himself?"

"Yep." She'd refreshed the water trough, and the long grass nearby meant he had plenty to eat. "Apparently they'd been looking for Harrison and Buddy when they didn't return."

She exhaled. What kind of man ditched his co-worker to play hooky with women he didn't know? The kind with a million ex-girlfriends, that's who. Ted hadn't been impressed. Until she'd mentioned Harrison was in the hospital, and why.

Not that she needed Harrison getting an even more swollen head with words like "hero" being thrown around. Maybe he'd been surprisingly brave in trying to help her as he had, especially for a man scared of snakes, but it wasn't like he owned Superman status as some of Hannah's co-workers seemed to think.

The drive didn't take long, not nearly long enough for the churning emotions to have a chance to subside. Heat balled in her chest, boiled in her stomach, and for some reason she felt awfully close to tears. The afternoon had been so good, the relaxing vibe just what her tense heart needed, then he'd shown up and spoiled things. Again.

"I'm so sorry, Hannah," Cassie said as the ranch house drew into view. She wasn't usually emotional, but she'd been up and down all day, and after the past hour, her emotions—along with the day—were fast spiraling out of control. "This certainly wasn't how I envisaged today going."

"It's alright. As long as you're okay and Harrison is fine, there's nothing to worry about, is there?"

She supposed that was true. "I just don't want this to have spoiled your day."

Hannah's hand clasped Cassie's arm. "The only thing that will spoil it is if my best friend is upset when there's nothing to be upset about. Of course, if Harrison was to get really sick, then that would be upsetting, but Poppy hasn't called to say that's happened, so it's okay to be okay."

In other words, pull yourself together and stop worrying. She lifted her chin. "Okay."

Hannah chuckled. "I have to admit, I'm looking forward to seeing what you've got planned for the next act."

Cassie groaned, then caught her friend's tease. "See? Now my plans will look so tame in comparison."

"I think after that episode we all need some tame time."

Probably. Sitting down and enjoying high tea while watching the 2022 adaptation of a Jane Austen classic was about all the drama she could sustain. Bree, an Austen aficionado from long ago, had mentioned Hannah was wanting to watch more girly movies, given her usual diet of strictly sports fare. And while this adaptation was scarcely historically accurate or faithful to the book, especially the heroine's characterization, it should still prove sufficiently romantic enough to woo an Austen newbie who'd never read the book and didn't know any better.

They soon entered the ranch house, and after greeting Mom,

who kissed Hannah on the cheek, Cassie shooed away Hannah to go sit in the living area. Poppy and Jess had previously decorated it with the rustic chic vintage theme that would be present in next weekend's wedding. That part of the house totally fit that vibe anyway. The low beams and wooden paneling and antiques and sepia photographs told the story of a family whose house had been built last century and expanded over generations to fit the changing needs of those who had lived here. She loved her home, even with its creaking stairs and cupboard doors that didn't always close according to the vagaries of the weather. This was home, and love colored the walls as much as any pine wood stain. Modern houses, like Franklin's apartment in the city, didn't hold nearly as much personality or character.

She moved to the kitchen and began helping her mom plate up the afternoon tea treats. Jess's arrival soon saw her help too, as the increased noise in the living area suggested everyone else had also arrived.

"Where's Poppy?" Mom asked.

Cassie exchanged glances with Jess. "She ended up having to go to the hospital."

Mom blinked, her eyes widening. "What's happened? What's wrong with her?" She moved to the key rack as if planning to get her car and go there too.

"No, no, it's okay! She's fine. She just had to drive someone there."

"Why? What happened?"

"Snake bite."

"A snake? We've hardly ever seen them around here."

Jess put her arm around their mom's shoulders. "It was a garter snake, so not venomous, and he'll be okay."

"He?"

Cassie drew in a long breath. And here it went. "Harrison Woods."

"Who?"

God bless her mom. She was so domestically minded.

Between running the house, helping Dad with the ranch book-work, tending the vegetables then canning and preserving their produce, and attending Bible studies with her friends from church, she rarely had time to watch TV or movies unless it was for Franklin's hockey games. That had changed a bit with Hannah's sports reporting role on ESPN, so Mom knew more than she'd ever thought she'd know about sports because Hannah had reported on them. But Mom did love *As The Heart Draws*, and had especially loved Tanner's role, so it would be interesting to see how she'd react once she realized one of her favorites had gone.

"He's with the show," Cassie admitted.

"What was he doing there?" Mom asked.

"An excellent question," Cassie mumbled.

Jess swapped looks with Cassie. "He thought we were in trouble and came to help."

"Then got bitten by a snake?"

There was another exchange of sister looks, where Cassie tried to communicate that in *no way* was Jess to mention Harrison had tried to help her out. There was no reason to give her mother the idea that Cassie had been in danger or that Harrison was in any way a hero.

"It was a garter snake, so he should be fine, unless he had an allergic reaction," Jess said. "I'm kind of surprised at the bleeding though. I think he might've cut himself on a stick, too."

"Oh my goodness!" Mom glanced at Cassie. "Will this affect the show? Was he important in it somehow?"

Cassie bit back a sigh, and avoided looking at her mom by washing strawberries at the oversized white ceramic farmhouse sink. "He should be fine. We'll know more once Poppy calls."

"But why is she taking him and not you if he's connected to the show?"

"Another good question. Did her baby sister like the man? Cassie shrugged. "Poppy wanted to."

"Oh, I hope he's okay."

"In the meantime," Cassie plastered on a smile, "we have guests waiting for drinks and food so we better go entertain them."

She grabbed two platters of savory treats then returned to the living area. Much more of her mom's interrogation and she'd soon crumple into unwanted tears.

The others were happily discussing their attire for next weekend, except for Hannah, who despite Bree's pleas, refused to share details of her dress. Cassie and her mom and sisters had been there when Hannah and her mom had bought it, along with the pale pink bridesmaid numbers the three of them would be wearing.

Cassie cleared her throat. "So, here is a charcuterie board, with some of your favorite cheeses, Hannah. And a fruit platter to balance it out."

Jess entered with a tiered plate full of sweet pastries, and old-fashioned treats like thumbprint cookies and meringues. "And sweets for the sweet."

"This is beautiful!" Bree declared.

That meant a lot coming from the hospitality queen. "Now, we have punch over there." Cassie pointed to the glass bowl set up on a table in the corner. "And if you feel like it needs a little something extra we have provisions so you can add it yourself." Most of the girls didn't drink, but Poppy had said some of Hannah's colleagues might like the option. "And we'll have hot tea ready soon, in case anyone wants that."

She took two orders for tea, and returned to the kitchen, where her mom was on the phone.

Her mother glanced at her. "Okay, well, thanks for the update, honey. We'll see you soon." She ended the call. "That was Poppy. She said he's been seen by a doctor and had medication and they'll be here soon."

She flicked on the kettle, her heart sinking. "They?"

Her mom nodded. "She's bringing Harrison here."

"Why? This is Hannah's afternoon, and he's already wrecked things by showing up completely uninvited at the creek."

"I said it was the least we could do after he'd been hurt trying to save my daughter." Mom's eyes held sparks. "Why didn't you say something?"

"Because it was unnecessary. The snake wasn't venomous."

"But how was he to know that? Cassie, I don't understand why you're so antagonistic to this man."

"That's because you haven't met him," she grumbled.

"Cassie." Her mom's inflection held the same layers of disappointment as when Cassie had plucked out the rooster's tail feathers or given Franklin a black eye as a kid. "That's not how we treat people."

She ducked her head. She knew that. *Knew* it. But despite her best efforts to rein in her tongue, she kept failing. *Lord, I'm sorry. Please help me.*

"Cassie."

Her mom's arms slipped around her and squeezed, and she rested there for a moment, letting love hold her, until she finally straightened, wiped under her eyes. "I don't know what's wrong with me."

"I know you've been busy, honey." Her mom stroked her face. "But don't let the outside pressures inside your heart. Remember Who you belong to."

She nodded, and sucked in a deep breath, releasing it shakily. "Do I look like I've been teary?"

Mom patted her cheek. "You look fine. And Hannah is enjoying herself. Hear that?"

Hannah's laughter floated from the living room, and hope filtered through her heart. Maybe this afternoon could be redeemed after all.

It soon grew apparent that this afternoon would not be redeemed at all.

No sooner had Poppy arrived, then the man himself was met with squeals and calls to "sit down" and "put your leg up" and "would you like something to eat?" and he was peppered with questions about his bite.

He glanced apologetically at Cassie—that was something at least—when her mother met him and insisted he eat something, cooing over him and glancing between him and Poppy like she'd finally found a potential son-in-law. Please.

Cassie glanced at the paused movie, frozen in a frame with the heroine in a ridiculous pose that wasn't in the book at all. Her gaze trickled to her glass of punch, as the murmurs continued around her. Why couldn't she be like the others here and simply be bubbly and sweet and something like the girl she used to be? The girl who used to tease and banter and be nice. Ever since this man had come along she'd felt extra tense, edgy, the kind of girl she neither liked nor wanted to be. And now, she had the strangest sense that she no longer fit in with these people, with her own family. Tears pricked. She blinked them back.

"Cass?"

She rubbed her face and stood. "Excuse me."

Ignoring the questions of whether she was alright, she hurried to the bathroom. No, she wasn't. Right now she felt all wrong, and staying out there, listening to the adulation he was lapping up, was likely more than even Mother Teresa could've mastered.

She gripped the sides of the stone vanity, wishing she could simply will strength to her emotions instead of this feeling of fragility akin to one of Mom's delicate teacups. This was ridiculous. Petty. Childish. And felt impossible to wade through.

A peek at the mirror wasn't kind, and required ducking into her room to apply the lightest mask of makeup to hide the red nose and eyes. There was no need to let the world know she'd been so close to crying.

But when she returned, it was to find that the Austen movie had been replaced with one of Harrison's own, an action/fantasy flick that he was offering explanations on, like he thought himself Tom Cruise providing a personalized director's commentary.

Suddenly the fact they were eating scones with jam and cream and drinking tea felt so incongruous. The high tea vintage vibes of before now felt so last century and old lady-like. What—so now he'd hijacked her best friend's bachelorette party? What more could the man do to wreck things?

Maybe she should go check on Buddy. Or find a quiet corner and down a pint of her mom's homemade honeycomb ice cream. It didn't seem she was needed here.

HARRISON GLANCED across the room to where Cassie sat poised, fingers gripping the arms of her chair like she was planning to flee. He hoped she wouldn't. Her presence was the only reason he hadn't argued harder when Poppy had insisted on bringing him here. Then, when Mrs. James had practically forced him to sit down, he hadn't wanted to be rude, so he obeyed, heart filling with gladness when he realized his position would be nearly opposite Cassie. He didn't care about the movie, only wanted to speak to her, try to get her to understand that the last thing he wanted to do was interrupt her time with her friends. But an injured man without a vehicle or a horse was at the mercy of others to get home, and he couldn't very well plead for the use of a car, not when everyone was being so kind to him.

Then she'd left suddenly. He'd wanted to follow but knew that'd look weird. And when some of the women had complained about the movie they were watching and asked about his instead, Poppy had insisted on finding one and pressing play. He'd then been forced to explain various things as they asked questions about this actor or that. Cassie's look of dismay when she returned had been enough for him to want to hike back to his room in the back of the barber's shop, but Bree had asked another question and he'd been duty-bound to answer.

He sipped from the glass that Mrs. James had plunged into his hand and swallowed overly sweet punch that reminded him of what his grandma used to make. His throat tightened. This house, this place, this family. This was what he wanted. He glanced around the room—he didn't like watching himself in movies—taking note of the aged furniture, the paintings of the Rockies, the pictures and photos of those he assumed were long gone family members.

He glanced at a nearby dark-toned wood frame holding a photograph of a pretty woman standing with a man, both dressed in the style of a century ago. He peered closer at the woman, his skin prickling. His grandmother had a cameo brooch like that. It was one of the few things he took with him wherever he went, a keepsake from a past he would otherwise prefer to forget.

"Harrison?"

He glanced at Jess, then realized how it must look with him staring at the photograph like a weirdo. "I just saw something that reminded me of one of my grandmother's possessions."

Cassie peeked across at him, as Jess said, "Your grandmother is still alive? Lucky you. Our grandparents have all died."

"She's dead."

"I'm sorry."

He shrugged. "Wasn't your fault."

Poppy snickered, which broke the mood as the other women joined in her laughter. But he was only conscious of the one who didn't, and how she didn't look at him, her gaze averted like she really didn't want anything more to do with him.

And he could understand that. But didn't know how to extract himself without adding further burden to an already crowded place of obligation.

He'd tried, but obviously had failed, to help Cassie. Just like he'd tried, and obviously failed, to help his mom. He might've saved his grandmother's cameo, but Mom had only owned it for a few months until her heart stopped, like she'd decided that with the loss of her marriage she had no strength to live for anything more. Not even her only child.

He glanced across at Cassie, but she kept her gaze away. Regret kneaded. His head lowered, and he traced the mud smudges on his jeans.

He wished he knew what to do that could make it up to her.

EIGHT

G rr.

Sometimes it was very hard to be a Christian. Rather, some *people* made it very hard to be a Christian.

Cassie sorted through the clothes in the costume section of the prop barn, searching for the apron that Ainsley had used last season. It was here somewhere. If only she could remember where it was.

But ever since the incident on Saturday afternoon, she'd struggled to hold any thoughts with great coherence. She'd enjoyed church yesterday, but most of her memories of the weekend centered on those few hours between laughing at the creek, celebrating Hannah, when everything was as it should be, then the drama of Harrison's unexpected arrival, and even more startling heroics when he'd saved her from a garter snake.

Her lips twisted. Of course, a girl didn't really need to be saved from a non-venomous snake, but the fact he'd leapt into action painted him in slightly different colors than how he'd appeared before with his whining about mice. Or maybe that had more to do with how his arms had felt around her, his body close to hers, when she'd been wearing nothing more than a swimsuit.

Dust motes floated as she shivered. She had never been more

thankful for deciding to wear her one-piece rather than the bikini that lurked in her closet. This whole encounter which already felt a dozen shades of awkward would have been ten times worse if she'd worn *that* little number Poppy had once given her as a dare.

It had been awkward enough anyway. Biting her tongue when the others had only wanted to talk about how brave Harrison had been, what a hero he'd been. Please. The man was scared of mice! Not that she was so ungracious that she'd told them about his mouse phobia. There was no need to add to their alarm about the ranch's critters.

And while it might've been more Poppy's fault that the man had returned to the ranch house after his hospital visit, he should've known not to give in—again!—to the others' requests for him to stay. Instead of poking fun at the Austen adaptation, all talk had focused on him and his movie career. Hannah had said she'd enjoyed it, and it was a day nobody would ever forget, so that was something. But Cassie's feelings were muddier. Yes, she resented the fact he'd stolen the show with his antics, but she wasn't sure if it was based more on his intrusion or the way he made her feel at the creek, when he'd held her in his arms.

She shivered again. There'd been that moment when he'd looked at her, his face soft, his gaze intense, which had sent a ripple across her soul, and definitely *not* made her feel like a good Christian. The ongoing feelings of resentment didn't either, but in a very different way. And now she didn't know how to manage any of these...emotions. Which meant the best bet was to stay away, stay out here, with only Miranda for company while she tried to get her act together.

Cassie winced. What was wrong with her that she was applying acting metaphors to herself? The man was a menace. Invading her afternoons, her thoughts, her peace. God might've reminded her to pray a blessing on him, but she sure didn't want to.

The door opened, and Poppy appeared. "There you are."

"Here I am." She pasted on a smile for her way-too-helpful sister.

"Whatcha doing?"

"Trying to find one of Ainsley's aprons for continuity from last year."

"For continuity? Who on earth remembers what she wears from year to year?"

"Apparently large numbers of her fans do." Cassie shrugged. "There are blogs devoted to historical accuracy in shows like this."

"Huh. I wish I could be so famous that people cared about my clothes," Poppy grumbled.

"The downside of that is that people devote blogs to all kinds of other things too."

Because she may have just seen a blog or two devoted to Harrison's hairstyles which had seen her fingers accidentally slip to search for one about his girlfriends, and what she'd read there was eye-opening indeed.

She knew from Hannah and Franklin's experiences that the internet could be a savage place. But there was a world of difference between the number of people commenting on a somewhat niche sport like hockey and the sheer volume who gossiped about Hollywood hunks.

Silence descended, which Cassie hoped would see Poppy reflect on whether she needed to stay. Unfortunately, when she finally looked up and met her sister's gaze, it was to see amusement in the blue-green eyes they'd inherited from their mom.

"So, have you seen him since?" Poppy asked.

"Seen whom?"

Poppy's lips curved. "I love how you want to pretend you don't know who I'm talking about."

"Um, I'm busy here, in case you haven't noticed."

"Fine. Pretend all you like. Is Harrison okay after his bite?"

She shrugged. "I guess so."

"You guess so?" Poppy's eyebrows arched. "Come on. The

man saved you from a snake, and you barely talked to him all Saturday. Don't tell me you haven't spoken since."

"Okay then."

"So you haven't?"

She shook her head. Perhaps she was behaving like a child, but she'd never liked being put on the spot like this.

"Wow."

"Wow what?" Defensiveness clawed up her chest. "I didn't ask him to be there."

"He saved you from a snake—"

"Unnecessarily," she muttered.

"—and then got bitten himself. Aren't you grateful?"

"Yes. But I still don't think it was needed."

"Man. What is your problem with him?"

Good question. One she'd been struggling with since their first encounter. "I don't like arrogant people."

"Come on."

"Or people who act entitled. There's something about the way that man walks into a situation like he's expecting the world to revolve around him that turns me off. Plus, I don't think he's a Christian."

"Just because he's not a Christian—and how do you know that for sure, anyway?—doesn't mean you can't still be nice to the man."

She pressed her lips together, conviction soaring.

"Do you know how embarrassing it was to have to try to explain your behavior while we were waiting at the hospital? The poor man didn't know why you gave him the cold shoulder. Did you even say thank you?"

Ouch. No, she hadn't. But still, "I didn't ask to be picked up. Some people would call that sexual assault."

Poppy's eyes widened. "Are you insane?"

"He should've asked. It's called consent."

"And when was he going to do that in the, oh, I don't know, millisecond before the snake struck? Cassie, Harrison was trying to help you, not harm you. He wasn't trying to kiss you or anything else. I don't know what twisted world you're living in, but you should've heard him. He was in pain, and couldn't understand why his good deed was going punished."

Cassie glanced at the lace-edged apron in her hands, her fingers ruffling the edges, shame filling her throat. Maybe there was something wrong with her, that she couldn't even thank him for trying to help. And while a garter snake wasn't venomous, he hadn't known that. So the fact he'd literally put his life on the line for her made her feel very small.

"Has he ever done anything specifically to you in order to upset you?" Poppy asked, more gently this time.

The fog of the past two days lifted, as a roll-call of his previous misdemeanors passed through her mind. He'd been annoying, sure. Thoughtless more than once, too. But he hadn't actually hurt her, physically or verbally.

She sighed.

"Is that the sound of 'no' that I'm hearing?" Poppy asked, way too incisively.

"You do know that as the youngest sibling you're not supposed to be asking questions like that, right?"

"I also know that as your sister who loves you, I'm duty bound to ask those kinds of questions to make sure you're not missing out on a good thing."

A good thing? Her heart tensed. Did that mean Poppy liked him? "If you like him so much then why don't you chase after him?"

"Oh, we don't like that, do we?" Poppy mocked. "Besides, there is no point chasing after a man who clearly only has eyes for someone else."

She swallowed her protest, sure any objection would only cause Poppy to twist the emotional thumbscrews harder. But Harrison couldn't like her. This wasn't grade school. Surely the man was old enough to know the way to the heart of a woman involved wooing, not pulling her ponytail in the hopes of getting her to notice him. And why he might like her made zero sense.

"I think you have rocks in your head," she finally said.

"I think you're trying to avoid the subject."

Darn tootin' she was.

"Look, I don't know why you'd be surprised he might like you —"

Yeah, Poppy said that because she hadn't witnessed Cassie's Oscar-level of grouchiness with him.

"—because you're a straight shooter, and that's probably really refreshing to a man caught up in the Hollyweird world."

"Yeah, what man doesn't want someone pointing out his flaws?" Mark, her handsome high school ex, sure hadn't.

Poppy shrugged. "Plus you're smart, and capable."

"Yep, that makes me a catch."

Poppy's hands found her hips. "Where is all this negativity coming from?"

She shrugged, although she had a fairly good idea. That's what happened when one stirred through the cesspool of remembered words from ex-boyfriends. Guys who decried her work ethic as freakish, or her godly boundaries as quaint. She didn't fit the mold most men required in a girlfriend these days. She probably would've suited the *As The Heart Draws* era just fine, though.

"Oh, and plus you're pretty."

"Gee, thanks." Super nice to have that tacked on the end like an afterthought. Even if it was more true about her than for either of her sisters. Poppy was classically beautiful, while Jess owned a vivaciousness that added sparkle to her looks. Cassie, in contrast, had always felt like the plain Jane of the James sisters. Not that she wanted her appearance to define her, but still.

"What are you doing here, anyway? Don't you have work or something?"

"I have Monday mornings off. And like I said, I wanted to know how he is."

"Well, if you go on set maybe you'll find him and you can ask him yourself."

Poppy pushed to her feet. "I might just do that."

"Great."

"Good."

Poppy stared at her a moment longer. "What is it you really object to?"

He was too different. They had nothing in common. Besides, he made her senses react in ways they had no business doing. Guys had always let her down before, and letting her heart off its leash guaranteed heartbreak again. But saying any of this was too hard. Best to just keep it simple. "He's not a Christian," she said flatly.

"Then what are you going to do about that?"

And Poppy smirked and flounced from the room.

Grr.

HARRISON'S STOMACH GROWLED, and he pushed himself up on his bed. He'd been grateful for time off yesterday and this morning that allowed him time to nurse his injury. After the hospital had agreed with Jess's assessment that it was a non-venomous garter snake, and the blood had likely been caused by a stick, he'd battled swelling which meant lying on his bed memorizing lines or watching TV for most of Sunday. Neither activity entertained half as much as his time at the Three Creek ranch house, time when he'd received more fascinating insights into the differing personalities of the James sisters.

He liked Jessica's practical, calm ways. He liked Poppy's directness and sense of fun. And seeing how they vibed off their elder sister showed another interesting facet of this woman he was becoming more intrigued with each day.

He couldn't forget holding her. Couldn't forget that moment of terror, followed by the moment of pain. Then couldn't forget how Cassie avoided speaking to him, avoided even looking at him, while Hannah and her friends had peppered him with all kinds of questions about the acting industry.

He would've been flattered, except for Cassie's avoidance. And now, with his leg swelling, he'd needed to have the planned shooting of outdoor scenes rearranged around him to focus on scenes shot in the schoolhouse. And he was stuck in his room, flicking between lame TV shows, while he avoided the giant leather-bound book positioned prominently on the bedside table.

The low production values of the made-for-television movie forced his eyes from the TV screen onto his phone. He probably should post more on social media. He took a picture of his room, trying to give as much of an aesthetic vibe without making it too obvious where he was. The guessing game about his latest role continued, but after the weekend, where between Hannah's friends and the hospital nurses who'd recognized him and asked what he was filming, he was fairly sure someone would be spilling certain beans pretty soon.

Tanner's final episode would air this weekend, so once the network's publicity department gave the all-clear it'd be safe to post the truth. It wouldn't hurt to have a stash of photos up his sleeve, ready for posting once news got out, especially if the fans were as rabid as Ainsley, Dana and Dustin had suggested.

He liked having fans but had never had rabid ones. And the fact this show had such a loyal following twisted his insides with both anticipation and terror. Some people—Lincoln Cash was one—appeared to know how to deal with that side of fame well. Harrison had never been that famous, the best he'd scored was a number five role billing status on IMDB, so to be a solid second, after Ainsley, was new territory for him. As was rabid fans.

He wished Cassie was more of a fan.

He still didn't understand why she seemed to hate his guts. What had he done that was so bad? There'd been that moment, before, when she'd stared deep into his eyes, when he'd really thought—

Knock knock.

He straightened from his position on the bed and used the remote to turn off the TV. Maybe this was her. "It's open."

The door swung open, and—

"Poppy? What are you doing here?"

The blonde smiled. "Funny. My sister just asked the same question."

His chest thudded. Cassie had?

Poppy held up a tray. "I bumped into your assistant—Maxine, isn't it? And she mentioned she was about to bring you your lunch, so I thought I'd offer to be the delivery girl."

"Aren't you thoughtful?" Delivering his lunch, taking him to the hospital, driving him back to the western town afterwards. Although he hoped it wasn't for any other reason...

"Right?" Another smile, full of sass. "Plus, I wanted to check on how you're doing."

He gestured to his bound-up leg. "It's still attached, so that's a plus."

Her nose wrinkled. "It still looks swollen."

"Too swollen for wearing boots, so I'm stuck here while they film stuff without me."

She passed him the tray, and he settled it on his lap. "Are you bored yet?"

"Not yet," he lied.

Her lips half-curved. "I don't know whether to believe you or not."

"What's with all the mistrust?"

"Exactly. That's something else I said to Cassie this morning."

His heart sank, and he pulled the tray of food closer to hide his dismay. Cassie didn't trust him?

"I hope it's all okay," Poppy said. "Maxine said this is your usual Monday order, but I don't mind going back and changing things if you want."

"Thanks, but this is good."

She pulled out a chair, and repositioned it to face him.

He lifted a brow. "Was there something else?"

Her mouth quirked again. "Maybe that's it," she murmured, as if to herself.

"What are you talking about?"

"Nothing." She shook her head.

Yeah, clearly not nothing.

"So, you're okay? Nothing else I can get you?"

"I'm okay, and thanks, I'll be fine."

"Is it okay if I pass that on to Hannah and the others? They've all been worried about you."

All except one of them, who clearly did not care for him, seeing she hadn't even thanked him, let alone bothered to check on his welfare. Heck, even Hector and Chuck, the security guards, had stopped by and offered their thoughts and prayers for a swift recovery.

"Um, yeah, go for it. But I'd appreciate it if you could remind your friends not to say anything about me being on the show."

"Sure thing." She nodded, and got up, pushed his chair back into position, tucked under the small dining table for two. "I should probably go, but I'm glad you're doing okay."

"Thanks for checking in."

"Of course. I know Jess will be glad too. Oh, and my parents said to say they're praying for you."

"Really?" He'd only met them briefly, but they came across as genuine, salt-of-the-earth people.

She nodded. "And even though she might not have said it to you, I know Cassie is grateful for your help."

"Mm." He'd believe it when he saw it. Which would likely be parked right next door to never.

"Seriously, she is. She said so this morning." She grinned again. "Among other things."

He knew that smile was bait, designed to make him bite. But no. He wouldn't do it. He wouldn't—

"What did she say?"

"Ha!" Poppy clapped her hands. "I *knew* you'd want to know." She moved to the door.

"What? You can't just say something like that and then leave."

"Can't I?" She opened the door.

Maybe she thought it was charming, but he was too tired and grumpy to be amused. "Have I done something to offend her? I really don't know what I've done wrong."

"You know, I'm not sure that she knows either. But if it helps, let's just say she's been a little stressed with everything lately."

"She's had a lot going on."

"She always does. She's a machine. She really needs to learn to relax. And now she's trying to do stock take and get the figures for the accountant." Her nose wrinkled. "Poor thing hates math like I do."

His heart flickered. "Maybe I could help. I'm okay with figures."

She studied him, then shrugged. "I can mention it to her. But if I were you, the place I'd really be looking for answers that will help is in that book right there."

"What book?" He followed her pointed finger to the leather-bound Bible. "Oh, that book."

"Yep, that one. The best book to read is the Bible," she added, in a singsong tone.

Reminiscences flashed. Church services. Sunday school. Memory verses. His grandma's voice: "We all need God, Harrison. More than anything. You need to stop running and let Him wrap you in His arms of love. Only then will you feel whole and complete again."

What was with these women around here peeking into his soul? Did he have a sign saying *Please comment on my spiritual state?*

His chest hurt, and he pushed himself upright, and picked up the chicken salad wrap. "Well, thanks again. Much appreciated." He fake-smiled, staring at her until she finally got the hint and left. As soon as the door shut, his shoulders slumped. He could feel a new ache beginning to grow, and this one was nowhere near his ankle. He couldn't explain it, but it felt closer to his heart.

NINE

Shadows were crawling across the buildings by the time Cassie had finally screwed up enough courage to make the trek into the western town. Her lips twitched. Riding in at this hour made her feel a little like a gunslinger from a spaghetti western. She already had the horse and the white hat. Obviously, she was the goodie in this scenario.

But even that was a thought she couldn't chase too deeply. She wasn't all that good. She'd been pretty selfish, allowing her insecurities from the past to get in the way of what Jesus would do. Jesus, who preached love for one's enemies, even if occasionally Jesus had also used a whip on some of them. Not that she'd be using any whips today. Her smile twisted, faded. For while Harrison Woods was not exactly her enemy she knew she definitely had some making up to do. Especially as the Holy Spirit hadn't let up from those feelings of conviction stirred up earlier by Poppy's words. The verse in Romans about "as far as it depends on you live at peace with all men" was now emblazoned on her soul.

Harrison might not be a Christian, but as one of Christ's followers she wasn't called to love only the lovely. And while

Harrison might qualify as handsome, he'd been definitely unlovely in some other aspects. But then, so had she.

Harrison wasn't like Mark. And just as Mark had arrogantly treated her, like she was dumb, so she'd been treating Harrison, like he had nothing to offer. Which wasn't Christ-like—or true—at all.

So, after finding Ainsley's missing apron, then continuing the tedium of stock take, then working on estimates for a cowboy-sci-fi mash-up movie, she'd known she needed to come here. Today. Well, tonight now. To apologize. To say thank you. And hopefully, forge a new path with this man who left her feeling so unsettled.

She knocked on the door. No answer. She counted to three and knocked again.

Then he opened it.

She swallowed, dragged her gaze from his bare chest up to his face. "Um, hi."

"You came."

His face, his tone, was soft, like he couldn't believe his eyes. Like he really had wanted her to visit.

She thrust the package in front of her. "I, um, came to say thank you for rescuing me last Saturday." Gosh, could her words sound any more robotic? "So, yeah. Thanks."

His mouth curved, as if he too recognized the extreme lack of gallantry in her manner. But she'd said what she needed to, and as soon as he took the peace offering of her mom's cookies, she could leave.

She shoved the package at him blindly, not wanting to look at the sculpted perfection of his chest again. She wasn't one of those girls.

His hand trapped hers, then drew around her fingers. Her breath hitched, then she tugged her hand away. "I gotta go."

"No, you can't."

"Excuse me?"

"You just got here. And I," he swallowed. "I'd like to talk to you."

Her insides tensed. He probably wanted her to explain her rudeness. Which would prove problematic as she couldn't really explain it to herself.

"Look, I said thanks, and I don't know what else there is to say."

"Have you had dinner yet?"

"What?"

"Have you eaten dinner yet?"

She'd snatched a piece of fruit when she'd called in at the ranch house to sneak some of her mom's cookies to give to Harrison. "Does an apple count?"

"No." He smiled.

Her heart fluttered, and she frowned to quash it. Okay, so maybe she was starting to see why some women liked him. The man had a certain appeal. A certain amount of *dangerous* appeal. She had zero desire to get sucked into falling under the spell of a handsome man. Not again.

"There. What did you just think of?"

"I beg your pardon?"

"You just frowned. I want to know why."

"That's a little forward of you."

"Is it?" He leaned against the doorframe. "See, I don't really know what it is that I've done to upset you, but it's clear that I've done something wrong, and I wish you'd tell me what it is."

Her stomach clenched. What was she going to do with a challenge put so bluntly? Everything he'd done seemed so trivial now. How could she explain in a way that didn't make her appear like a petty child?

"Whatever it is I did, I didn't mean to upset you, and I'm sorry," he said softly.

His apology, with that note of sincerity that made her think he actually meant it, met her own remorse, which spilled out to say,

"I'm sorry, too. Truly." She scuffed her boot on the dusty step. "And it wasn't you." Her sisters' words reared up, shaking the truth from her. "I…I've probably been over-committed with a few things, like my brother's wedding this weekend, and I'm not handling things like I should, so I've let silly things become bigger than they warrant."

"Hey, we all do that at times." His voice grew raspy. "I just hate feeling like I'm someone that people are trying to avoid."

He thought that? Her heart fisted. This must be why God wanted her to come here to apologize. How awful that her actions had made him feel that way. But apologies were only spoken air if there was no behavior that proved one's heart was changed. She was going to have to try harder. "I'm sorry. I…" She shook her head, as emotion appeared from nowhere, like a glacier avalanche, and she pivoted on her boot, and hurried away.

"Cassie, wait."

She paused. What kind of person would she be to make an injured man chase after her? Especially an injured man who had gotten injured because of her? Ugh. She was such a terrible person. She turned and faced him again. Somehow between the door and here, he'd managed to locate and put on a shirt. Thank goodness. Heaven forbid anyone had seen her with him shirtless in the shadows of the western town like this. They'd likely be thinking they were having a tryst.

Her shudder at that thought sharpened her word to hold a bite. "What?"

"Look, I just want you to know that if I have done something to upset you, I hope you'll forgive me."

Her heart stilled. Forgive him? She held back a sigh. What choice did she have as a Christ follower but to follow the Lord's command? "Of course."

"Can we be friends?" He held out his hand.

"Friends?" Now that was pushing things. She eyed his hand, then her gaze trickled back up to him. "I don't know how to be friends with Hollywood people."

His hand fell. "I'm pretty sure it's the same as with anyone else."

Was it? But when you scarcely saw a person, and their lives were splashed across the TV, how could you have any real connection? But then, her thoughts swung again, the same could likely be said about Hannah, and Cassie had managed just fine this past year to stay in contact with her...

"Besides, aren't you friends with Ainsley?" he persisted.

"I wouldn't dare to presume to call us friends. I like her, she's really sweet, but I'm pretty sure she just thinks we're acquaintances. It's not like my friendship with Hannah."

"That's not how Ainsley sees it. She stopped by earlier after her scene and mentioned you'd helped her out today."

"That was nothing."

"I've heard her say how much she appreciates spending time with people who are honest and real, and go the extra mile like you do."

Really? Her chest glowed. "I didn't know that."

"So now you do."

How crazy to think someone like Ainsley might think of her that way. Harrison was probably exaggerating—actors told stories and embroidered truth for a living, after all. "Well, thanks for telling me."

He smiled. "You're welcome."

Silence stretched between them, until it was broken by the screech of a bird. Was that what he wanted to say to her, or was there more?

"So, if you're friends with Ainsley, then maybe you could be friends with me too?"

His question slammed into her chest like a runaway train, propelling her back a step. "But...but that's different."

"How?"

"She's a woman."

"You don't have male friends?"

"Not really."

Although that was perhaps untrue. She was friendly enough with her brother's friends and teammates, people like Mike Vaughan, and Tom Chavez. They were nice enough, and those two were at least Christians, even if Mike was married, and Tom was often hanging around Jess whenever events drew them into the same circles. She bet he'd be asking Jess to dance at Franklin's wedding this weekend.

Which reminded her. "I need to go."

"You can't stay a little longer?"

She shook her head. "It's my brother's wedding this weekend and I still need to get lots of stuff done." Like oil the pews in the chapel tonight so they'd have time to dry and not stain anyone's clothes on Saturday.

"Is everything coming together okay?"

"It will." Especially if God gave her an extra five hours each day. Or she didn't sleep. "I, uh, bet you're glad to get a long weekend. Are you going away?" She mentally high-fived herself. See? She could do nice.

"Yeah. I still don't know where I'll go. I'd wondered about Banff."

"That gets pretty busy in summer, so you might need to book ahead. But you've got the whole weekend off, plus the Canada Day holiday on Monday. Why wouldn't you go see friends or family?"

His face closed.

Oh. Her heart softened. That said a lot.

He cleared his throat. "Poppy mentioned you were busy doing stock take or something."

She groaned. "Don't remind me."

He shrugged. "I was good at math, and could help if you like."

Oh! That was unexpected. Maybe the man wasn't like Mark, after all. "Thanks, but I got it sorted." His face fell, which hurried her to add, "But I do appreciate the offer. Really."

His lips tweaked into an almost-smile as he nodded. "Well, I know you're busy, so I don't want to hold you up." His palms faced her.

"You wouldn't be the good guy if you did that, would you?" She tipped her hat like the hero in one of those old westerns.

He appeared to catch her reference to a hold-up as he chuckled. "Or a friend?"

His tentative intonation and raised eyebrows held an invitation. One she wasn't sure she would be wise to explore. Because how could a woman be a friend with a man without emotions getting in the way, sooner or later? What would Jesus do? *Lord?*

She swallowed. Nodded.

His smile broadened, edged with what looked like relief. "Well, thanks for keeping me from being too lonely."

Her heart twisted. But she had to stay strong. She might have agreed to be friends with the man, but no way could she afford to get sucked into this man's charm.

"Have a good night, Harrison."

"It'll be a better one now." His half-smile arrowed straight to her chest again, leaving her flustered.

So she turned on her heel and mounted Ginger, and rode quickly away, without a backward glance.

The rest of the week passed, and while she hadn't gone out of her way to avoid Harrison, God was kind to her and ensured that either she or Harrison were busy elsewhere. She'd half expected to see Harrison around the western town on her way to supervising the setting up for the chapel, but Lance had said the leads were off shooting promotional, now that Harrison's leg was better. Which was just as well, considering all the prep that needed to be done for the wedding.

But now, standing here in the chapel's opened front doors on Saturday morning, she knew all her hard work had been worth it. Everything looked perfect. The chapel was beautiful, all vintage looking in soft whites and mellow timber. The pews had been freshly oiled, the roses stood in vases on their pedestals, the white drapery interspersed with pine leaves and twinkle lights. Everything was just as she'd imagined.

She smoothed hands down her jeans, hoping her hair would stay neat under its scarf. Honestly, she could almost channel Audrey Hepburn with this get-up. From the chin up, anyway. In a few moments, she'd take the ATV back to the house where she'd get changed into the dusty pink gown, a halter neck like what her sisters were wearing as bridesmaids. She'd snuck away just to double-check, half wondering if Harrison had left as he'd said he would, or whether he'd lingered. But no. He'd gone, along with nearly all of the rest of the cast and crew, just as the contract had stipulated. Only Hector remained on site, guarding the gate to the backlot.

Oh well. She squinted up where a cloudless sky promised heat, meaning the old-fashioned parasols that she'd sourced from the prop barn would be appreciated. They stood ready in another vintage umbrella stand, along with a sign painted by Poppy that declared "Ladies, please help yourself" in an olde-worlde font.

She glanced at her phone, winced, but paused to take a few quick snaps, before gunning the ATV and roaring down the western town's dusty main street, past the white tent and caterers, and over the hills and back to the ranch.

"All good?" her dad asked, as she rushed through the door.

"Looks great." She gestured to his suit. "So do you."

He winked at her and she raced up the stairs.

A quick shower later, then she was in her dress, and Poppy was smoothing her hair as the makeup artist wielded her magical brushes and sticks. Hannah had already had her makeup done and was getting pictures by the barn, and Cassie and her sisters would join her as soon as this was done.

"Whoa." Cassie's insides sparked as she finally glimpsed her reflection.

"You like?"

"I love." She smiled wryly at the makeup lady. "I know I've never looked this good before."

"It's all about enhancing one's natural features and creating a little bit of drama."

Her chest tightened. A tiny part of her wanted Harrison to see just how good she could look. She quickly snuffed it. Today wasn't about him. And while she might've agreed to be friends—well, sort of agreed—it didn't mean one should take a selfie and send it to a man, like an announcement about what he was missing. She didn't have his number anyway, so that was that.

"Come on, stop staring at how beautiful you are in the mirror." Poppy grabbed her hand. "Let's go take some pictures!"

"It all looks so beautiful," Sylvie, one of Hannah and Bree's friends, said. Cassie had come to know Bree's friend last year when Sylvie had come west to help when pregnancy had adversely affected Bree's health. Sylvie had gone north for family reasons of her own, so Cassie hadn't spent as much time with her lately. But it looked as though the snarky Goth girl had gone through her own transformation recently. Even though her tattoos were still on display under the dark blue chiffon dress, she appeared softer, somehow. Or maybe that had something to do with the reason she was holding onto the arm of Edmonton hockey player Ryan Guillemette.

Cassie smiled. "We've gone for rustic chic."

"And did I hear that *As The Heart Draws* was filming here recently?"

Her heart tensed. "Yes, it's been exciting."

"And Harrison Woods is staying here?"

Oh, who had spilled the beans? She really hoped it wasn't someone from last weekend. "Mm hmm."

"Cassie?" The minister—from Franklin and Hannah's church—needed her attention.

"Excuse me."

A short time later Cassie was standing at the front of the chapel, watching as her brother pledged his life and devotion to Hannah, his soft expression filled with love. She was pretty sure she'd seen him wipe away a tear when Hannah entered the chapel, escorted by her mom.

The stained glass of the chapel's altar window filtered rose and gold over the happy couple, the place filled with prayers and consecrated love. This was what love looked like, anchored with patience, kindness, hope. Franklin and Hannah had certainly had their ups and downs, but it had shaped them, readying them for this moment where they promised each other forever.

Her gaze swept the congregation members, so many of them in couples, or families, all smiling, as if remembering—or imagining—their own wedding days. Bree and Mike Vaughan. Brent and Holly Karlsson. Jai and Allie Mullins. Chris and Diana Thomas. Ryan and Sylvie. The hockey players that Franklin had come to regard as his Christian brothers, who stood with him while he pledged his life to Hannah.

Her heart tugged. She wanted that too. Someone who loved God and who loved her. A face flitted through her mind. She instantly batted it away. He neither loved God nor her. And while he might say he wanted to be her friend, everything felt too weird and uncertain and impossible. There could be no future, even if God did do a miracle and somehow drew the man to Himself. She blinked, hitched her smile up another peg, and refocused. Today wasn't about herself, or anyone else, but making sure Franklin and Hannah's day went as smoothly as possible.

After the ceremony, and yet more photos, it was time to go to the large white tent set up just outside the western town.

She glanced around the space, the laughter, the chatter, the smiles. Gratitude filled her heart. Everything was going on without a snag.

"You've done such an amazing job," Hannah said, as their main courses were cleared away. It would be time for cake soon.

"Thanks for all you've done. You're the best, sis." Franklin squeezed her shoulder.

"You're only saying that because somebody is over there chatting up Jess and Poppy." She gestured to where Franklin's teammate, Tom Chavez, was laughing with both girls.

"I'm not, because I really do appreciate you. We both do, don't we sweetheart?" He kissed Hannah's cheek.

Hannah smiled. "It's been a dream come true. I can never thank you enough, Cassie. I don't know how you managed it with everything else you did."

She barely had, but, "God was gracious, so it's all good."

"Amen, and amen." Franklin's brow furrowed as he glanced at Tom.

"What's wrong, honey?" Hannah asked him.

"Do you think he's interested in one of them?"

"I think big brother might need to keep an eye on them." Cassie smirked.

He cocked a brow. "Do I need to keep an eye on you too?"

"As if."

Hannah's smile held mischief. "Have you seen anything more of a certain person who-shan't-be-named?"

"Whoa, now this sounds interesting." Franklin's eyebrows pitched up. "Are you talking about the actor at your girls' event last weekend?"

Franklin knew?

Hannah's look held an apology as she murmured, "I didn't mean to tell him, but I don't like us to have secrets, and I figured he should know in case anything got said about last weekend. I didn't want any whispers about a Hollywood actor at my girls' afternoon tainting things."

Fair enough. She glanced at her brother. "And no. He's not a Christian, so you don't need to worry."

He nodded, but his head tilt said he wasn't convinced.

But he didn't need to worry. Neither did she. Not about a

certain actor, and definitely not about the reception. Everything was going so smoothly.

Her heart swelled with satisfaction as the dancing commenced. Hannah and Franklin were wrapped in their happy bubble, murmuring softly to each other. Her parents were dancing together, Jess was talking to Tom, while Poppy, the most graceful dancer on the dancefloor, was dancing with another of Franklin's teammates.

She glanced at the table where Franklin's hockey friends were placed. Most of them were dancing too, except for Luc Blanchard, who was sitting by himself, tugging at his bowtie like he couldn't wait to get out of his suit. She'd heard him declare—several times —that nobody would catch him dancing as he didn't want to squash some poor woman's toes. She smiled. She bet Poppy could make him boogie.

She studied her parents, then her sisters, then Franklin and Hannah again. And while she felt a sense of relief that this was now done there was also a degree of sadness that it meant her family had changed forever. Not that she didn't love Hannah, and wasn't glad about her joining the James family, but it was yet another sign that things would never be the same.

Who'd be next to marry? Maybe Jess. She and Tom had certainly hit it off. Poppy didn't seem too interested in any of the guys who tried chatting her up. As for herself...

Her aunt had asked her that question earlier. Cassie had responded with a peppy-sounding "Nope, I'm still single and happy to mingle."

But was that true? Maybe she should check out a Christian dating website. She knew several of her college friends had found love that way. There was a new one, Dream Match, which apparently specialized in helping singles in rural areas find someone with shared interests. Shared interests, like a heart for God, would be a good start. Even if it obviously ruled out some people completely.

Who knew that a man could get so bored of luxury living?

Harrison studied the view of Lake Louise, the famous aqua-blue lake pictured on a million calendars. Heck, the photos could've been taken from his lavish suite's balcony. A dream, a complete contrast to how he'd grown up, in that hovel nobody in Hollywood had ever heard him mention. His agent had agreed that Harrison's past could be airbrushed a little. Or a lot. Like, completely.

But now that he thought about it, it wasn't the leaky ceilings and bathroom plumbing that had been the problem. It was more the lack of connection with his family, the lack of love. Mom had loved Harrison's dad, but hadn't fought hard enough for her son. His grandma might've loved him, but she'd also died too soon. And Harrison's dad had only ever really loved himself, despite what his new girlfriend might think. You couldn't put a price on healthy, non-dysfunctional love.

And now, despite these fancy digs, he felt a similar yearning for more. No, not more gold-plated fixtures, but a yearning for those bonds that tied people together. Like what he'd witnessed last weekend at Hannah's bachelorette party. Like he could see between Cassie and her sisters, Cassie and her parents. He wanted that same sense of connection.

For what good was a view like this if there was nobody to share it with? Nobody to reminisce over the fine dining, or go hiking or swim with. And while the hotel had done their best to keep his stay private—although he bet their instant upgrade to a suite when he'd given his name was designed so he'd post about it on Instagram—the fans had soon found him. Which left him feeling a little trapped, like he couldn't go anywhere without people whispering about him.

And no, he sure didn't want to sound like he was complaining. Yes, the western town barber's bedroom had a cozy rustic charm, and was plenty comfortable, but it wasn't exactly chateau suite luxury. Yet he couldn't help compare this hotel to the wide open spaces on the ranch, and the feeling of freedom there. The fact that there, he could climb a hill and see no sign of humans, and feel a sense of peace, just himself and nature. Contrast that to the fact it was peak tourist season here, and even though they were surrounded by wilderness, there were just so many people, talking in a hundred languages. Simplicity and ease felt like a million miles away.

Or maybe that uneasy feeling was exacerbated by the questions roaming through his heart since last Monday.

He drained his water and leaned forward, elbows on knees, head in his hands. He closed his eyes, shutting off the famous view, as his mind tracked back to when he'd last spoken to Cassie. She'd no doubt appreciate this place, this view. And while her brother might be a well-paid hockey star, and her family couldn't be doing too badly if they owned ten thousand acres of prime cattle country, he wondered if she'd ever stayed at a place like this.

But he bet she'd more appreciate the beauty of nature than the million-thread bedsheets or the fact the waiters called him sir. She didn't seem to want that stuff, instead taking pleasure in simple things. And that fact drew him as much as her eyes, eyes that held more than a hint of the color and depths of the lake just outside his window.

A groan escaped. He didn't want to be attracted to her. She might appeal, but how could a life ever work out between them? She was committed to the ranch, to her family and work there. He lived out of a suitcase, traveling wherever the next role took him.

But something about her, and her family, made him greedy to want more. Maybe there was a way he could put down roots and finally find a home.

His fingers clenched, as he remembered her question, about why he didn't want to take advantage of a full weekend off and spend it with friends or family. Truth was that he had none. None that were genuine. His friends were mud-puddle deep and about as constant, only checking in on him when something was reported on E-news. And what did it say about a man when even his own father, the father who used to mock him for playing make-believe, now only talked to him when he wanted money? What kind of man did that?

He didn't want to play pretend with his dad, nor the woman he was currently with. How could he pretend to like the woman who'd broken his mom's heart and sent her to an early grave? Harrison sure didn't have enough acting chops for that.

What he wanted was the cozy family he'd witnessed at the Three Creek ranch. He'd instantly sensed the affection between them all, a tight unit of love, of what family should be like. That's what he yearned for. Someone to love, someone who could tease and relax with him, who smiled at him like she did with her sisters and friends, someone who didn't play pretend but was solid and real and smart and hardworking and every shade of wonderful.

He wondered what she was doing now, how her brother's wedding had gone, what she'd worn, what she looked like, who she smiled at, danced with, more.

He tugged at his hair. Rolled his shoulders. Stretched to relieve the tension.

But why was he still even thinking this when she'd barely agreed to be friends? She hadn't even looked back when she'd trotted out last Monday, like she didn't pay him another thought. She probably hadn't, which meant all of this was just in his mind.

Loneliness must be sending him mad.

He glanced at his phone, counting the hours until his stay ended. He couldn't wait to return to the ranch.

And to Cassie.

TEN

Anticipation filled Cassie as she rode Ginger through the western town, checking over the site before filming began today. It was amazing how much lighter she felt with the wedding over. Franklin and Hannah were now in Fiji, the reception tent and chapel decorations were down, and the western town looked exactly as it ought to represent the past one hundred and fifty years.

Yep, not a speck out of place to show that a hundred or so guests had been partying the night away just three nights ago. Most of the cast and all of the crew had returned, the only ones missing were those cast members not scheduled for shooting scenes today. Which meant Harrison was somewhere, as he was supposed to be filming today.

But...how silly was she to look for him, to still think about him when it was clear he wasn't for her. Put it down to feeling alone on the wedding weekend, even when she'd been surrounded by people, and the talk of love that had filled nearly every conversation

Mom had noticed, asking Cassie how she was feeling. She'd admitted to relief that everything had gone smoothly, even though she hadn't admitted to all of her emotions.

"I imagine that you'll feel something of a letdown after all the energy you've put into making this so special," her mom had said.

Cassie had nodded, and sure enough exhaustion had hit hard on Sunday. A nap and wedding cake leftovers and early nights for the past two evenings had helped with some of that. But the flatness had lingered, even as she tried to remember to be thankful, to count her blessings. Hopefully life could resume a slower pace now that all the wedding frantic-ness was done.

With no sign of anyone—no, she wasn't looking for anyone specific—she nudged Ginger along the road and up the hill, taking the path to the trailers and dining hall. She stopped in, saw Annie, got a coffee, but didn't linger beyond exchanging pleasantries with a couple of people.

Ainsley was one, her "great to see you" holding a sincerity Cassie now recognized as genuine.

"Did you enjoy your long weekend?" Cassie asked.

"It's always great to see my family."

"Where are they?"

"Just outside Vancouver. But enough about me. Tell me about your brother's wedding. I saw a couple of pictures on social media and it looked amazing."

Cassie smiled. "It was awesome. Everything went as planned, and I'm so grateful that God gave us good weather."

"Good weather sure helps with outside events."

"Just like with filming, hey?"

"Absolutely. So, tell me what you wore. I bet you looked beautiful."

"I have to admit it was one of my finer moments."

"Okay, I need to see a photo. Have you got one?"

"Of me?"

"Of course of you. I saw one of the bride and groom that Hannah posted—we follow each other on Instagram—but I want to see one of you."

Okay, then. Cassie pulled out her phone, showed Ainsley the photo that Bree had taken when Cassie had been standing at the front of the church, her face in profile as she smiled at Franklin while he'd pretended not to tear up. The light from the stained glass added a softness to her features, her upswept hair and makeup and fancy dress making her look like she was ready to feature in her own starring role.

"Oh, Cassie. You look gorgeous."

The thought that someone as beautiful as Ainsley Beckett describing Cassie as gorgeous drew gladness around her heart. "Thanks. I don't wear dresses too often," she confessed. "I was just relieved I was able to walk in high heels."

"I love your dress, too." Ainsley zoomed in on the picture. "So pretty."

"Pink isn't my usual speed, but it worked."

"As did that style of dress. Ooh la la."

She smiled. Yes, the cut of the dress had done her figure plenty of favors.

"Is that a photo of you?"

Cassie stilled, and went to retrieve her phone, but she couldn't very well snatch it from Ainsley's hand. Not when Ainsley was showing it to Harrison, who whistled.

"Oh, sorry, Cassie." Ainsley winced. "I should've asked. I get so used to showing others my own pictures."

"It's okay," she murmured, peeking at Harrison. Why hadn't he said anything?

"Doesn't she look gorgeous?" Ainsley prodded him.

His gaze lifted from the screen and met Cassie's. She swallowed at the intensity in his eyes.

"Really beautiful."

"Th-thanks."

"I mean it."

Ainsley softly chuckled as she handed back the phone. "I think he does. I don't think he's once said that about me," she confided, adding a wink for good measure.

"Maybe he just needs someone to prompt him the way you did for me."

"I didn't need prompting," Harrison said to Cassie, a slight frown in his eyes now. "I do think you're beautiful. And not just when you're all dressed up."

Her throat cinched, her chest growing tight.

"And that sounds like my cue to leave," Ainsley murmured, slipping away.

Cassie couldn't look away even if she wanted to.

Harrison angled himself closer, blocking out the increased bustle in the dining tent. "I missed you this weekend."

Her mouth was still dry from his first compliment. Her brain could barely cope with any more. Did he truly mean these things he kept saying?

"Did the wedding go well?"

She nodded. Swallowed. Found enough moisture to say, "I don't know if it makes me a bad sister or friend to say I'm glad it's over, but I was really relieved when it was all done."

"And everything went smoothly?"

Another nod.

"But of course it did. You worked so hard, I'm not surprised."

Huh. No criticism of her work ethic? Her defensiveness dropped a little more. "And you? Did you enjoy your weekend?"

"It was okay."

Only okay? "Where did you stay?"

"Fairmont Lake Louise."

"Fancy."

"It was nice, but not the same as here."

"I bet." Deserts could form by her tone. "Once you stay at the barber's, well, it's all downhill from there, right?"

His lips curved. "I missed you, Cassie."

Her breath hitched. He couldn't mean that to sound quite like that. "Well, lucky for you, here I am again."

"Lucky for me." His voice held a rasp.

She stepped back. If she didn't know better, she'd be almost inclined to think the man liked her or something. Which was ridiculous. Why would he like her when he could have his pick of Hollywood?

Besides, just because a man might say smooth things didn't mean a girl needed to believe them. And this girl couldn't afford to believe them, or allow her heart to get involved. She'd gone that way before, and it hadn't ended well. Besides, he wasn't a Christian. Was he?

"Why are you looking like that?" he asked.

She needed to go. But also felt a weird prompting to introduce some element of God into the conversation. Because Poppy was right. How could any non-believer ever know about God if Christians always kept their mouths shut? *But what do I say Lord?*

"Cassie?"

"I, um, I don't know. Uh, what do I look like?"

His smile twisted. "Like you're trying to figure me out. Which I'm cool with by the way. And I could help you out with that if you let me take you to dinner sometime."

Her breath suspended. "You said you wanted to be friends."

"And don't friends do dinner together sometimes?"

"Not male and female friends who are both single. At least, I've never done that."

"Maybe you should."

Part of her yearned to take him up on his offer, to know what it would be like to live in this man's world for a moment, to be the pretty thing on a handsome man's arm. But another part urged caution, and because she was trying to listen to the Holy Spirit more these days, she knew she had to obey that prompting more than anything that tugged at her heart. And she had to make something very clear.

"I don't think I could have dinner alone with a man unless he was a Christian."

His face shadowed for a moment. Then he tilted his head. "Who said anything about being alone?"

Ouch. Had she just misread that and embarrassed herself some more?

Either way, this conversation felt like she was playing with fire, and she had no desire to get burned. "Have a good day, Harrison."

"You too, Ms. James."

She nodded, then hurried out of there, itchy with awkwardness.

That night, she returned to the ranch house early to find her youngest sister frantically packing. "What's going on?"

Her mom looked up from where she was stirring green beans, ready for a casserole. "Poppy got a call from her friend Bailey, you know, the one she worked with at the dance school in Winnipeg? Apparently she got some amazing opportunity that means Poppy is catching a flight at 7:30pm."

"Tonight?"

"Yes."

"What kind of opportunity requires that?"

Her mother shrugged. "I don't think Poppy even really knows. But it's happening and it's now or never, which is how that world seems to be."

Like the world Harrison lived in. His world wasn't like hers, bound by the age-old rhythms of the seasons. His was frantic, fast-paced, snatching at his big break when it came, not tied to anything, not grounded, not like her at all.

Her heart panged. See? Too different. It could never work. "I'll check if she needs a hand."

She went upstairs and asked Poppy what she knew.

Poppy shrugged. "Bails asked me, and she sounded panicky, which made me feel panicky, because she's usually so perky and cool. But I had some summer classes cancel so I could make it. And in this industry, opportunities pass, they don't pause, so when they come by you have to do all you can for your chance to get noticed. So I'm helping Bails out while she gets her big chance."

"Is there anything I can do?"

Poppy straightened, her suitcase crammed full with clothes. "Help me shut this monster?"

Cassie chuckled, and struggled to zip it while Poppy sat her petite backside on the top cover. "I don't know anyone who has as many clothes as you."

"That's because you and Jess"— Poppy gritted out as she helped tug the fastener—"are tomboys."

"Although according to Ainsley Beckett, I scrub up alright."

"Scrub up?" Poppy's nose wrinkled. "Who on earth says that? I bet Ainsley didn't."

"Well, no. She said I looked gorgeous," Cassie said as meekly as she could.

Poppy grinned. "And you did." She finished zipping with a flourish and a "Victory!"

Temptation filled her to share what a certain somebody else had described her as. But that would only fuel speculation, and after the last encounter between Cassie and Harrison that Poppy had witnessed, she had no wish to invite more.

Especially when she'd clearly misunderstood things. Embarrassment writhed. Had he thought she was angling for a date? She blinked the memory away. Refocused on her sister. "You're a good friend to Bailey."

Poppy grinned. "That I am."

Friend. The word propelled her thinking straight back to the someone she really didn't want to be thinking about. How had she misjudged his invitation to dinner? Had it been so long she'd forgotten the cues and secret clues of dating?

Poppy paused. "What's wrong?"

"Nothing."

"Clearly not nothing. Come on, spill."

She shook her head.

Poppy's gaze narrowed. Then she went to the top of the stairs. "Mom? You don't need to miss your Bible study now. Cassie just said she's taking me to the airport."

"What?"

Poppy smirked. "You're taking me to the airport, and you're gonna spill the tea."

She exhaled. Poppy might be the youngest, but there was a reason she'd earned the name *Bossy Poppy* from a young age. "Fine." Besides, her sister might be able to offer some perspective.

Thirty minutes later they were on the highway heading to the airport, and Cassie had finally found the courage to admit what had been said. But she'd never admit who had said it.

"Do you think if a man asks a woman out to dinner that it means he's interested in her?"

"Yes." Poppy turned in her seat to face her. "Why? Did someone ask you out?"

"I don't know."

"Clearly you do or we wouldn't be having this conversation."

"Well, I thought that's what he meant, but then he'd said he only wanted to be friends, and now I don't know what he means."

"Cassie!"

Cassie braked. "What?"

"No, keep driving. I don't want to miss my flight. But I honestly don't know why you didn't share this earlier. How come all the good stuff has to happen when I don't have a chance to get all the juicy details?"

"There are no juicy details."

"I beg to differ. You need to tell me who, what, where and when."

"I'm not telling you who."

Poppy nodded. "Which can only mean it's Harrison. Am I right? Or are my Poppy vibes off?"

"Your Poppy vibes aren't off," she mumbled.

"I knew it!" She clapped her hands. "I could tell he was really into you at the creek. We all could."

Oh dear. "Then I don't understand. Why did he say what he did?"

"Well, you better now tell me everything he did say."

Cassie reported the conversation as best as she could remember.

Poppy winced. "Poor guy. But you know he was just trying to save face, right?"

"Um, no. Was he?"

"You said that bit about only going out with a guy who was a Christian, so then his next comment was all flippant, like he didn't care. But he cares."

A shiver rippled through her. She flicked the turn indicator as she steered into the exit lane for the airport. "But he's not a Christian."

"So don't go out with him." Poppy shrugged. "But you can always pray for him."

But praying for someone knit them closer to a person's heart. "I don't think that's wise."

"Don't you want him to become a Christian?" Poppy demanded.

Put like that, well, "Yes."

"Hey God," Poppy prayed aloud, as Cassie drove into the departures lane for domestic flights. "We ask You to touch Harrison right now, wherever he is, and make him aware that You are real, and that You love him, and want to have a relationship with him. Whatever is holding him back, please deal with it right now. In Jesus' name, Amen."

"Amen," Cassie echoed, surprised at the force in Poppy's tone. It'd been a long while since she'd heard her sister pray with such conviction.

"Look out!"

Cassie jerked the car to a halt, as an elderly man jay-walked in front of them, bag trundling behind him.

"And that is why God created pedestrian crossings," Poppy yelled out the window.

"He'll hear you," Cassie murmured.

"I doubt it. He's old."

But from the way the man looked at them, then made a rude gesture, his hearing worked just fine.

Poppy snickered, as Cassie moved to the drop off zone. "I hope he's not on the same flight as me."

"I bet he's thinking the same." Cassie parked, popped the trunk, then opened the door. She only had a minute before the parking patrol officers would tell her to move on.

Poppy grabbed her bags. Then caught Cassie in a hug. "Thanks so much."

"Have fun. Let Mom know when you arrive. I'll be praying for you."

"And I'll be praying for you, sis." Poppy grinned. "And for him."

Cassie nodded. And now, so would she.

⌒

CASSIE'S WORDS chased Harrison through the day, causing him to flub some lines.

"Come on, Harrison," Mal snapped. "Get your focus. Where's your head at?"

"Sorry."

But seriously. She didn't want to go out with him? Would only go out with a Christian man? Wow. He'd only had a handful of rejections in his time, but never something that felt so cold.

It was dusk by the time Mal called cut, and he was released to his meal. He was entering the dining room just as Brenda, the stuntwoman who often doubled for Ainsley, exited. "Whoa!"

Brenda flinched, and a soul tremor recognized that action. His mom used to do the same.

"Sorry, Brenda. I didn't see you there."

She tugged down her sleeves. "It was my mistake."

"Are you okay?" he asked softly.

She bit her lip, and his gaze fell to her wrists. Wrists ringed with big dark bruises.

"What happened?"

"It's nothing. I fell."

He nodded slowly. Those bruises didn't look like any that might be expected from the rough and tumble of a stuntwoman's role. "My mom often 'fell' like that too. Usually when my dad hurt her."

Her gaze veered sharply to him. "It's not like that."

"I hope not. Because I know how terrible it was in my family, and I wished my mom had found the courage to leave him. Nobody deserves to be beaten. That's not how a man should treat anyone."

"It's not like that," she repeated stiffly.

"Okay. But if it was, then I hope you'd know that I'd be happy to do whatever I could to help."

Her bottom lip trembled. "He only does it when he's drunk."

"That's no excuse." He softened his tone. "If you need help, I'm here."

She jerked a nod, then rushed away, the episode leaving him unsettled. He hoped she'd stand up for herself, that she'd find a way to be stronger than his mom had ever been. He couldn't see Cassie ever letting a man control her like that.

Cassie. His thoughts shifted as he thanked Annie for his food, as he twirled his fork through his spaghetti. He hoped she'd had a good day. Even if she'd made it clear they'd tap out as only friends.

"This seat taken?" Ainsley smiled at him.

"Is now."

She got her meal then joined him at his table, their late finishing scene meaning most of the others had left, and they could eat alone. His lips twisted. Ainsley had no problem with eating with him. And she was a Christian. So what was Cassie's problem?

"Hey, are you doing okay?"

He looked up.

Ainsley's brow had puckered. "You looked happy this morning, then something happened and you've been off your game."

He shrugged. "I'm fine."

"No, you're not. What's wrong?"

The concern in her voice made him swallow a lump along with his pasta. "You're a Christian, right?"

She nodded.

"So why is it okay for you to eat with me, while...others don't want to?"

Her head angled. "Others? I'm afraid I don't understand."

He really didn't want to have to explain things. Already this conversation felt like he was in quicksand. "Would you go out with a non-Christian?"

Her eyebrows shot up. "Are you asking me out?"

"No."

Her shoulders relaxed. "Good."

Good?

"Not because I don't think you're nice, but because it's my policy not to date coworkers. And yeah..." She winced. "I've dated non-Christians in the past, but I'm starting to believe that God only wants me to date Christian men."

"But why?"

"Because the Bible says not to be yoked with unbelievers."

He exhaled. The Bible. His old nemesis. He thought of the big book next to his bed. "You don't seriously believe everything you read in that do you?"

She nodded.

"What, even the eye for an eye business?"

"You know the Bible?"

"My grandma used to take me to church."

"Oh, God bless her," she said softly.

Well, yeah, Amen. "But that's not answering the question."

"About not dating non-Christians?"

He nodded.

She sipped her apple juice, eyed him carefully. "I think God wants us to be careful who we give our hearts to. He wants His people to be blessed and enjoy satisfying, life-giving relationships, and if two people want different things, then there will always be tension."

"But not if they love each other."

"Love?" Ainsley's eyebrow ascended. "I thought we were only talking about going out for dinner."

"I did too, but it looks like it's about a lot more than just food," he grumbled.

"Is it Cassie?" she asked softly.

He glanced away, jerked his chin.

"Oh, she's gold."

"Gold who won't go out with me," he complained.

"And she said it's because you're not a Christian?"

He nodded.

"Well, good for her. She's trying to do what God says. Do you really want her to go against her conscience and convictions?"

"Of course not. But I'm not a bad guy. I don't understand what the problem is."

"I think you should probably talk to her."

"Yeah, like she'd admit the truth," he scoffed.

"Okay, well, here's my two cents. I think for a lot of Christian women it's because they see dating as more than just a meal out but having a relationship with someone who has the potential to be part of their future."

"You mean marriage?"

She nodded. "I know a lot of people may think that's old-fashioned, but there's something to be said for waiting until you can see if someone else's values align with yours before embarking on a relationship. Jumping in too quickly can lead to a lot of frustration and a lot of broken hearts." She smiled without cheer. "Ask me how I know."

He didn't need to ask. He'd seen the gossip magazines and speculation on TV about Ainsley's love life. And while he knew not to pay gossip rags much mind, she had been involved in a few high-profile relationships over the years that had not ended well.

"And to be honest," Ainsley continued softly, "I think God

wants to protect us from more brokenness. So when it comes to something as important as who we give our hearts to, who we might potentially share a future with, then it makes sense to give it to someone who shares our values and interests and the things most important in our lives. And if you're a Christian, then God and doing things His way is supposed to be the most important part of your life. So it doesn't make sense to give your heart to someone who doesn't think that way. That person would always be wanting your attention when sometimes God needs it more." She smiled wryly. "I don't think I'm explaining this very well, and like I said, I'm still figuring a lot of this out myself. But I can now see the value in waiting for a Christian man who loves God and wants to do things God's way more than his own."

Harrison stared at the remnants of the tomato-based sauce congealing on his plate. Well, that ruled him out.

"Can I ask a personal question?" Ainsley asked.

"Sure."

"If your grandmother took you to church, did you ever make a commitment?"

"A commitment?"

She nodded. "Did you ever ask Jesus into your heart?"

His lips rolled in as he thought back. "I don't know. Maybe? But I used to believe in Santa Claus too, so I don't think that would matter."

"Shh! Some of us still believe in Santa." Ainsley's teasing smile reminded him that she'd played Mrs. Claus in some Christmas movie not too long ago.

"You know, I've said this before," her head tilted as she studied him seriously, "but Harrison, I believe God loves you, and wants you to know Him. He's your heavenly Father."

He tensed. "Don't say that. I hate my father."

The words hissed through space and time, as a kaleidoscope of images and words and remembered bruises begged for attention. Maybe people around here never admitted such things, but he couldn't play pretend right now. He wasn't that good an actor.

"Oh, Harrison." Ainsley's face was soft, and—was that a tear? "God isn't like your dad. He's perfect. He loves you. He wants your best."

He shook his head. "I can't believe that."

She was silent, her posture slumped, then she straightened. "Well, I'm going to pray that one day you can."

He rose to leave. She could pray all she liked. It didn't mean prayer worked.

Eleven

A strange urgency to pray for Harrison chased Cassie home from the airport, accompanied her evening meal, followed her to sleep. The man needed God, anyone could see that, and it sounded like God was on his case.

The next day she didn't see him, which was good, as she didn't know what she'd say. But she did see Ainsley who looked at her in a way that suggested Harrison might've shared with her too.

"Cassie? I, um, hope you don't mind, but Harrison mentioned some things you said the other day about dating—"

She tensed. Oh dear.

"—and we ended up having a really good conversation about God—"

What?

"—and anyway, I hope you don't mind that I stepped in."

Cassie blinked. "Are you serious? You talked to him about God?"

Ainsley nodded.

Wow. "You've done better than me."

"I think it was your stance about not going out with a non-Christian that really got him thinking."

Oh. Oh! "Well, that's good."

"I'm praying for him," Ainsley said.

"Me too," Cassie admitted.

Ainsley was called away, and Cassie's phone rang with a query about an upcoming booking. She dealt with that, then checked with Lance about whether she was needed on set anymore. She'd really like more time before she was placed in a position where she might see Harrison and feel obliged to talk to him again. Fortunately, the crew were able to go on without her help, and she could help her dad with haying instead. Time with him was just what she needed instead of the constant tumult of questions and confusion.

"You know I employ others, Cassie," her dad said. "You don't have to put your hand up every time there's a need. You deserve a rest after all your hard work last weekend."

Maybe, but spending time with her godly father and his quiet nature allowed more time to pray, something she did as she refocused on tying down tarps over the stacks of hay.

Yes, she could admit it. Harrison attracted her. And no, it wasn't just his smile or abs or anything like that. Something within her sparkled to life in his presence, their banter providing anticipation, and dare she say even some ease and joy, in their encounters. Maybe there was some truth to those rumors about opposites attracting, after all.

But while she could admit herself susceptible to the man's charm, it didn't mean anything more. It couldn't, not while he wasn't walking with God. And even then, the tangle of motives for wanting him saved added to the clutter in her heart. *Lord, forgive me. Help me to want Harrison to find You for his sake, not my own. Touch his heart with Your love, Lord.*

Her phone chimed—some parts of the ranch had excellent reception—and she dug it out to see her sister's name lighting the screen. "Jess?"

"Hey, want to come and stay with me for a night or two in the city?"

"Why?"

"Because."

"Because why?" she asked suspiciously.

"Because I'm staying here in Franklin's place and I could really do with some company. And didn't Hannah give you a nice voucher to spend at a spa here?"

She had. And maybe Dad was right and it would be good for her to get away. Between the planning for the wedding and all the ranch things of late, the idea of getting a few days of quiet—even if it was in the city—sounded like heaven. "Um, sure. I'd need to check the schedule, and see if Dad needs my help, but I might be able to swing it."

"Great! I do think that while Franklin is away us kitty cats should play."

"I'm not sure if that's how that expression is meant to go."

"I don't care. I've been working with animals all day and I think I'm turning into one. So you can see my need for some sanity and a sister who might need some time out."

"Franklin does have a well-located apartment." Near restaurants, and movies, and galleries. Effective distractions, all.

"And it would be a shame if it was not being appropriately appreciated while he's away."

"I'll talk to Dad now."

"Great! Hey, do you think that Poppy would like to come too?"

"She might, but she's in Winnipeg."

"What's she doing there?"

"Bailey needed her for something."

"Oh, to have a job where you can just drop everything," Jess teased.

"Right? Then there are those of us who find it super easy to walk away from the cows and fences and stuff."

"You have a hard life, that's for sure."

"You know it."

But the idea of getting away, of hanging out with her sister, another person who could talk sense and bring clarity, sure held a lot of appeal.

"I'D FORGOTTEN how much fun this is!" Cassie grinned at Jess across the restaurant table. Below them, the lights of Calgary gleamed as the sky tinted with orange and pinks of the setting sun. If a girl was going to go eat fancy food with her sister, then this revolving restaurant located in the top of the Calgary Tower was the place to do it.

"I'm loving this black truffle fondue," Jess said, dipping a skinny fry into the cheesy pot.

"Thanks Franklin, for your generosity." Cassie clinked glasses with her sister.

Franklin and Hannah's gift voucher was part of a thank you gift to Cassie for organizing their wedding. She hadn't minded cashing it in tonight, even if the truffle-flavor of the fondue was a little strong for her liking. Everything else was perfect. Everything else yesterday and today had been perfect.

The past day of sleeping in and being free of responsibilities had been just what her mind and body needed. Watching dumb movies on Franklin's large screen TV had been a treat too. She'd love to see his face at the recommendations that would start popping up on his account after what she'd been viewing. Another part of her wondered if he'd realize that a number of those movies had starred a certain Mountie impersonator who was currently living at Three Creek's western town.

But watching Harrison, in the privacy of her own—well, Franklin's—space was good. It only reinforced how a man who had played a himbo in a *Baywatch*-like show, the hot guy with a different girlfriend each week, was so wrong for her. That even if he wasn't immediately disqualified by his non-Christian status, he would be by his roles. Sure, it wasn't like he had ever played a sex-crazed vampire or psycho killer, but he'd played enough roles that made her hesitate some more. Like, how much kissing did one actor actually need to do? The thought that a man who looked like that and had said he wanted to take her out for dinner made her wonder where else he'd like to take her.

She glanced around the dining space. "Do you feel a little conspicuous, being the only two female diners when everyone else is a male-female couple?"

Jess shrugged. "I don't care."

Cassie eyed her sister. "So, um, has Tom ever taken you any place like this?"

"Tom?"

"Tom Chavez? You know, the Tom who is always talking to you any chance he gets."

"Oh, please. We're just friends," Jess scoffed. "Besides, I don't know if Franklin would want one of his teammates going out with his sisters."

"Why not?"

"Because it's got the potential to mess things up if it goes wrong," Jess said matter-of-factly, before eating another fry.

Huh. Jess had clearly thought this through. Which meant that she wasn't perhaps as non-aware of Tom as she might like to portray. Which meant it was her big sister duty to say, "But what if things went right?"

Jess gave another half-shrug. "To be honest, I don't really have time for a relationship right now. I'm snowed under with work, and I have to work as much as I can to pay off my loans."

Cassie winced. "I bet you're thankful for the scholarships you received." As the smartest sibling in the James family, Jess had received more than a few awards over the years.

"So grateful. But hey, I don't mind working, even though it would've been nice to spend the day with you, instead of dealing with more cats and dogs." Jess sipped her virgin margarita. "You'll appreciate this. I even got to deal with a python today."

"Yeah, no. Not super appreciating that."

Jess laughed. "So, how is the handsome hero?"

Honestly, it was like her sisters were related the way they

carried on sometimes. "He's fine." That was safest to say. He probably was fine, anyway.

"You know he wasn't the one responsible for changing the movie at Hannah's girl's afternoon."

He wasn't?

Jess eyed her. "That was Poppy."

"Oh." Her gaze dropped to the white tablecloth. Maybe he wasn't as self-absorbed as she'd thought.

"Some of the other women weren't loving the non-period appropriateness of the movie, so they were happy enough to change it. And Poppy was happy enough to oblige."

Her heart knotted, and she peeked up. "Do...do you think she likes him?"

"Poppy? Like Harrison?" Jess blinked. "You mean as more than just a friend?"

Cassie winced, hating how her question had exposed her. "She did spend an awful lot of time with him that Saturday, driving him to the hospital then back home."

"She did that because somebody else wouldn't."

Jess could melt glass with that gaze. Cassie didn't have the heart to justify why she hadn't.

"Besides, I don't think it would matter if she did." Jess's lips curved.

No, Jess wasn't implying what she thought she was, was she? Although hadn't that been exactly what she'd wanted to know? Oh, how had she gotten stuck in this no man's land of ambiguity? Where had straight shooter Cassie gone? She swallowed, then finally admitted, "He asked me to have dinner with him."

Jess didn't seem one bit surprised. "And?"

"And I said I wouldn't have dinner alone with a man unless he was a Christian."

Jess clinked her glass against Cassie's. "Good for you."

"Yeah, but since then I've felt bad. Like, I'm trying to stand up for my values, but this world does not make it easy."

"Sure doesn't." Jess's gaze held steady. "But it's a good thing we have a God who understands that, and gives us grace and strength when we need it."

Oh, she needed it.

Cassie was thankful for the waiter's interruption as he asked if everything was satisfactory.

"It's great, thank you."

She glanced out the panoramic window. The restaurant had rotated to now show a different view, one reaching beyond downtown's high-rise buildings and stretching through the prairies to where the peaks of the Rockies could just be seen. Where the ranch was. Where the western town was. And where a certain man was. The man she'd watched on TV today, and a man who desperately needed Jesus. *Lord, touch him.*

HARRISON GRASPED the bouquet in one hand and knocked on the door. She'd already called him forward, but this was taking things to a whole new level. But after the past few days of questions that forever circled in his brain, he needed to finally ask them or go insane.

And now, it was Friday evening, and with the shooting schedule meaning he'd gotten off early, he'd arranged for Maxine to pick up these flowers so he could deliver them himself.

He took a delicate sniff. He hoped she liked wildflowers. They didn't smell like some flowers he'd given women before.

The door opened, and Mrs. James appeared. "Harrison?"

He cleared his throat like a nervous schoolboy. "Hello Mrs. James."

She smiled. "Leonie, please."

"I, uh, wondered if Cassie was at home." Her car said she was.

"Oh." Her gaze dropped to the flowers then lifted to him. "I'm afraid she's not here. She's been in the city the past few days."

In the city? Doing what? There with whom? Was she on a date—with a good Christian man? "When does she return?"

"On Sunday, after church."

Church. Of course. He should've known.

By then these flowers wouldn't look as fresh and would be fit for the trash. "Um, is Poppy here?" She might appreciate flowers as a thank you for all the driving she'd done for him.

"I'm afraid you're all out of luck. She's in Winnipeg helping out a friend."

He thrust the bouquet at her and smiled his most charming smile. "Well, these are for you. To say thank you for your hospitality on that day I got bitten."

Leonie took the brown paper-wrapped bouquet gingerly, and smiled. "I'm sure the original intended recipient would still like them when she returns."

"No, don't tell her." He took a step back. "I don't want her to know."

"But she'll see them, and ask questions, because heaven knows my husband hasn't given me flowers in thirty years."

"Oh." His heart sank. "I didn't realize that. He should have, though. I mean, given you flowers."

She chuckled, fortunately. "That's what I've said more than once." She gestured for him to come inside. "Would you like to join us for dinner? It's just me and Derek tonight."

"I shouldn't. You two probably would like to spend the night together." He winced at how that sounded. "I mean—"

"We've spent plenty of nights together." Her eyes twinkled. "But if you're trying to say we should go on a date then I'm afraid we don't do that very often either."

"Well, tonight could be the perfect opportunity."

She shook her head. "Not for a man who gets as exhausted as he does. Besides, Derek says he prefers my cooking to anything he can get in a fancy restaurant. And when we can have the best Angus steak in the province here, why spend a fortune paying to eat it somewhere else?"

Good point. "He sounds loyal."

"He is. I'm very blessed. Derek is such a good man, a faithful husband, and a loving father."

Harrison's heart prickled.

"And I don't mind if you're here to explain why I suddenly received flowers from a handsome young man, even if we both know I'm not who he came to give flowers to."

"I shouldn't."

"You should. We'd like the company." She turned, leaving the front door wide open, leaving him no choice but to follow down the hallway to the kitchen.

There they found Derek James, who shook Harrison's hand, even as he eyed the flowers Leonie held. "Pretty flowers."

"Harrison got them for Cassie, but gave them to me because she's not here."

"Cassie, huh?"

The rancher's assessing look straightened Harrison's shoulders. "I wanted to talk to her, but Leonie said she was out."

"So he's stuck talking to us instead." Leonie winked at Derek, which drew a small smile. She turned to Harrison. "Are you a steak man?" Her brow furrowed. "You're not vegan or anything like that?"

"I like my meat." Good thing it was true. Otherwise he sensed there'd be no hope to win any points with Cassie's parents who ran a beef cattle ranch.

Derek nodded, then invited Harrison to get a beer from the fridge. He declined, but took a zero-sugar Coke instead.

"You don't drink?"

"No." He swallowed. "My dad was an alcoholic, and I've grown up not wanting to be anything like him."

"I'm sorry that was your experience."

Harrison shrugged. "It's life. But I guess I've learned that everyone can take responsibility for their choices."

"Not everybody does though."

"True."

The conversation triggered memories of when he first arrived and complained about so many things, blaming others. Was it any wonder that Cassie didn't want anything to do with him? He sighed.

"What is it, son?"

Son. Emotion pricked his eyes, clamped his throat. For so many years he'd longed to feel like someone's son, to feel part of a family, that it took a while to answer. Then he realized just what Cassie would think of him poking his nose in again, peeking into her world. She'd hate it. She'd hate him. He needed to leave. Now.

He rose. "I'm really sorry, but I just remembered I need to go."

"Are you sure you can't do that after you eat?"

The scent of frying garlic and onions was nearly more than he could bear. "I don't think she'd like me being here."

"Who? Cassie?" her father asked.

He nodded.

"What are you? A man or a mouse?"

Right now he felt a lot like the latter. Which finally reminded him of yet another Cassie encounter where he'd fallen short. "I'm sorry. I—"

"Son, sit down."

He obeyed.

"Harrison, what is it that you really want to know?"

And like a geyser spilling a lifetime of dirt and gunk, out it all came.

Harrison's desire to make amends with Cassie. Ainsley's comment about being unequally yoked. His questions about God. The truth about his past. He probably got way too real and raw and honest, and there were times he saw Leonie bite her lip and Derek frown that tempted him to veer from honesty. But he sensed this was a rare moment in life that had been handed to him and he could either live the rest of his days with these questions or could finally ask someone who seemed pretty wise. And even though some of his questions involved Derek's daughter, he was considerate enough to answer them.

Three hours later, he realized that maybe this was why he'd felt a prompting to get the flowers and come here tonight, and that it wasn't because of Cassie, after all.

"So I can sit here and tell you all kinds of things, son. But it's best you read it yourself." Derek yawned.

"I'm sorry. It's late."

"Hey, this is a conversation worth staying up for." Derek smiled wearily. "But I do have an early start tomorrow."

"I'll go."

Derek grabbed his arm. "But not before I pray for you." He closed his eyes, and Harrison figured he'd better do the same. "Heavenly Father, help this young man see that You desire a relationship with him. Help him to know Your love, the real love of a Father unlike any he's ever known. And thank You for Your promise that those who seek will find. We pray this in the mighty name of Jesus. Amen."

"Amen," Harrison whispered.

"Now, you've got those verses? Look 'em up. And keep seeking. If you go in with a closed mind that's exactly what you'll find as it'll all feel closed off to you. But if you're truly wanting answers, then you know what to do."

He swallowed. Nodded. Thanked him for his time. "Please tell Leonie I really appreciate the dinner. It was delicious."

"You're welcome, any time," she called from the hallway, dressed in a quilted robe, not unlike one his grandma used to own.

Maybe that's why he went over and hugged her, but after a moment's freeze, she didn't seem to mind, patting him on the back while he tried to find composure.

He exited immediately, not wanting them to pity a man whose eyes threatened to spill at any moment as emotions toyed with him. Despair that he'd likely just killed any chance of them accepting him wrestled with concern at what Cassie would say when she knew what had happened tonight, while a faint hope beckoned that he might finally be on the right path.

THE WESTERN TOWN was silent by the time he returned. The sensor security lights helped light the way, so he found the back of the barber's easily. He unlocked the door, went inside, and sat on the bed and toed off his shoes. The Bible sat there, goading him.

But then the memory of what Derek had said, and the memory of what his grandmother used to say, urged him to pick it up. So he did, opening the front cover, spying a dedication to Cassandra. He traced the name, wondering if this had once belonged to Cassie, and if so, had she put it here for him to read. That thought instantly felt self-indulgent, so he flicked over a few pages until he found a table of contents.

It had been a long time since he'd read a Bible, but he knew the book that Derek had mentioned was towards the back, so he turned there. As the pages flicked over he recognized names. Matthew, Mark, Luke, John. The book of Acts. Romans. First Corinthians. Then the next.

The words that Ainsley had said, that Cassie had implied, that Derek had mentioned, about not being yoked with unbelievers. It was there in black and white, in the seventh chapter. The next chapter reminded of the importance of being holy, avoiding sin, of repentance. He flicked back another page, read chapter five. The reminder to live by faith, not by sight. The plea to be reconciled to God. The declaration that for a believer "anyone in Christ" was a new creation, the old had gone, the new had come. He could see how this linked with the last verse in the next chapter, where God said "I will be a Father to you and you will be My sons and daughters."

A Father. A loving Father.

He flicked over to the next book, Galatians, and found the verse Derek had said could be found in chapter three, that promised that all believers were considered children of God because of faith. Then in the next book, Ephesians, the first chapter again reiterated that God had predestined people to be adopted as His sons because of what Jesus had done.

And as he read the verses Derek mentioned, something stirred deep, deep within.

It was clear, and perfectly summed up in the verse his grandmother had loved, how God had sent His son Jesus into the world to save sinners. That God offered mercy. That it was a matter of faith, of believing, but when one did, God wiped the slate clean and made a man a new creation. That God wanted people to live holy, wholly to Him and His ways.

He could kind of understand Cassie's objections now, and what Ainsley had tried to say. He already knew how fame or fortune or alcohol or dysfunction could blind a man's eyes to the truth. His father's legacy and rejection were not a fair representation of who God was, and Harrison would be shortchanging himself and his future by continuing to think otherwise.

He swallowed. His heart was whirling, thoughts swirling, memories at war with the promise of freedom and hope for the future.

And wetness splotted the page as he slipped off the bed and sank to his knees and lowered his head and prayed.

TWELVE

Four days away from the ranch had left Cassie feeling like a new woman. That was, until she arrived home, saw the bunch of flowers sitting in a place of pride on the dining table, and discovered who had given them.

"Harrison came here?" Cassie asked. "You invited him to dinner?"

"We couldn't leave the poor man to eat alone," her mom said.

Those last two words triggered an avalanche within. "Yes. Yes, you could have. He's used to eating alone."

"That's not very kind Cassie. Especially when he came here to give you that beautiful bunch of flowers."

"He said that?"

"Near enough."

She stroked the petals. If asked to describe her ideal bunch of flowers, it would look pretty similar to this. A mix of wildflowers, dusky apricot roses, Queen Anne's lace, and stalks of lavender, it looked and smelled divine. Clearly the man had paid attention to what she might like. She shivered. Had any man ever gone to so much trouble for her before?

"He's thoughtful, Cassie."

"He's still not a Christian, Mom."

"Not yet."

"What do you mean not yet?"

Mom smiled. "Your father might've talked with him some, might've explained about a few key passages to look up in the Bible."

"Really?" The skepticism loading that word could sink a ship.

"Don't take my word for it. Go find the young man yourself and ask him."

But if she did that, and he said he was, that might crack open the door to a future she hadn't dared imagine. Couldn't dare imagine. Because even if a miracle occurred, and Harrison did find faith, how could a relationship work between two such opposites?

And while part of her was tempted to ride over there right now and demand answers, another part urged caution. She had lived a lot in her emotions lately, and didn't want to keep doing the same. The sermon at church this morning had convicted her about whether she was walking by faith or walking by sight. She knew a lot of what she'd been doing in recent weeks had been because she'd been so busy she had focused on the wrong things. Focused on what she could say, on what she could do, while forgetting how extraordinary God was. God, her heavenly Father, who loved to bless His children with good things. Had busyness snarled her heart so much that she'd forgotten about God's blessings? Maybe it was time to let go, to trust God to lead and guide her, to sink into the rhythms of God's grace.

She exhaled. It was way past time to do so. *Lord, forgive me for thinking I have to do and know it all. Help me follow You and Your leading. Whatever You want Lord, whoever You've got for my future, help me to trust You with it all.*

She closed her eyes, glad for this moment of stillness, glad the clutter of past weeks was gone and she could more easily hear the inklings that just might be God's whisper.

And she prayed again, knowing this next task would need God's strength.

BY THE TIME she reached the western town the shadows were falling. The day's heat still lay in the timbers and dust, and she was glad when she reached the barber's. But her knock went unanswered, and she felt a degree of disappointment. Where was he?

"Hello?" she called cautiously. "Harrison?"

Still no answer. Huh.

She kicked at the dust. The ranch was so large he could be anywhere. The day had been warm, so maybe he was down at the creek. She didn't want to go looking there, though. Maybe she should turn back.

A faint sound drew her down the side of the building to the front. Then to look down the main street. At the end, down at the chapel, there came the faint sound of...music?

She frowned. Nobody was supposed to be in the chapel; there was no filming scheduled there today. So who was there?

The singing got louder as she drew closer and her agitation rose as she mounted the steps and pushed open the white doors then—

"Oh!"

Harrison turned, then stabbed off his phone. Instantly the singing ceased. "Um, hi."

"What are you doing in here?" Her gaze flicked down and she realized what he held. Her old Bible that she'd placed in his room. Her heart pounded. "What are you doing, Harrison?"

He straightened and looked at her. Offered a small smile. "I could ask you the same question."

She blinked, her mind awhirl. "I heard you were looking for me."

"Did you have a nice time in Calgary?"

Her chin dipped. "Did Mom tell you where I was?"

"Yes."

Was no part of her life to be kept from this man? "Mom said you had dinner with them."

He shrugged. "I actually went there to have dinner with someone else, but she was away."

He meant herself, didn't he? But the second-guessing regarding Poppy and whether he might hold the slightest interest in her prettier dancer sister made her ask, "Who?"

"You know who."

"Say it."

His eyes fixed on hers. "You."

Connection flowed between them, drawing her chest tight, her heart to beat faster.

"But you weren't there and so your mom felt sorry for me and invited me in."

"She has always had a thing for strays."

He flinched.

Remorse bit. "I'm sorry."

"I guess that's fair. I know I've been in your space a lot, but..." He swallowed, looked down, his lips pulled in.

For a moment she thought he was going to cry.

Her heart softened. How she hated this high horse of indignation she sat on. The man was obviously feeling vulnerable and here she still was, six guns blazing.

He glanced up. "You don't know how lucky you are. With your parents, I mean. Well, that, and growing up here. Having a family who loves you."

Compassion drew her chest tight, tickling the backs of her eyes. Oh dear. If he kept this up, she might start to cry. She swallowed and gestured outside. "It's a bit cooler outdoors. If you want to talk, that is."

His lips twisted then he nodded, picked up the Bible and his phone, and passed her. She closed the door, and joined him on the porch, sitting near but not too near. She peeked across.

Harrison stilled. Swallowed. Then, gazing straight ahead, said in a low voice, "My dad kicked me out of home as soon as I finished school."

Cassie's heart panged. But she couldn't offer a word of sympathy. If she spoke, he would certainly shut down this rare moment of vulnerability.

He hunched forward, hands gripping the edge of the porch's wooden boards, and she had to strain to hear his next words.

"I'm a disgrace to the family. That's what he told me. That I'm weak, too soft playing make believe, not doing a real man's job." He peeked across at her. "He'd probably prefer someone like you to be his son rather than me."

"Excuse me?"

He shrugged. "Because you're good at all the things he values. You can fix pipes and bathrooms and you can ride a horse like a boss—"

Wow.

"—and you're tough and smart and pretty and everything I'm not."

Whoa. Okay, so maybe she didn't need to jump on the high horse of offense and go riding for the hills. But more than taking pleasure in the fact he thought her pretty—was he for real?—she recognized his comment for the plea it was.

"I'm sure your dad loves you, and is proud of you," she assured.

"Yeah, you'd think he might be, but it's hard to believe that from a man who burned my birth certificate."

She felt her eyes widen. "No way." How could any father do that to his son?

"Way," he rasped.

"Oh, Harrison." The poor man.

His body froze, and it wasn't hard to deduce how he'd interpreted her words, as if her sympathy was too much. But she couldn't let him continue this way. Her hand found his and gripped it.

He glanced at their joined hands, and she realized what she'd done. Moved to tug her hand away, but he tightened his hold.

Her heart fluttered, but no, she knew he didn't mean anything by it. Neither had she. Holding hands with a famous actor in this moment was simply a moment of offering comfort, of offering support, like she would with anyone else. Well, actually, with most other people she'd be hugging them by now, but that would definitely be giving this man the wrong impression. So hand holding it was.

She silently prayed for him, that God would comfort him, and somehow bring restoration in his family. Harrison might act tough, but the rasp in his voice showed he wasn't immune, that his father's burning of Harrison's birth certificate was like the ultimate act of rejection. And now she knew this, she could understand why he kept aloof and didn't let people in. The fact Harrison had admitted this to her felt like a miracle, like a gift of trust had been handed to her, something she would hold carefully, like a treasure. That they continued to sit here, holding hands, undisturbed, felt like another miracle. Not that it was one she'd ever prayed for. But with the set so busy, the fact he'd had time to share something so personal, something that obviously bothered him, felt like she'd been walking in God's plans and purposes, here at exactly the right time God needed her. Even if she was only here to provide comfort, and nothing else.

Nothing else. She stilled, now acutely aware of how hot her hand was, that it was feeling a little sweaty, even. And her skin definitely wasn't soft and delicate like Ainsley Beckett's probably was. Although whether Ainsley had such amazing qualities as the ability to fix bathrooms remained to be seen...

She drew her hand away, then inched back, before subtly wiping off the sweat down her jeans. No. She wouldn't go giving him the wrong idea.

He cleared his throat. "And anyway, that's why I appreciated talking to your folks. Your dad was real understanding. He answered a whole bunch of my questions about all kinds of things." He peered at her, as if wondering if she knew.

"I haven't spoken to them about that."

His shoulders relaxed, as if he was relieved. Which made her wonder exactly what he had been saying.

"Anyway, ever since you made that comment about not wanting to go out with someone who wasn't a Christian I've been wondering why. So your dad explained some things, and I came back to my room and found the Bible—"

Her pulse escalated.

"—and I might've been reminded of some things my grandmother used to say. She was a God-fearing woman and took me to church when I was young. I lived with her for a time after my parents split up. Anyway, I found the verses your dad mentioned, and yeah." He swallowed. "I might've prayed, and given my heart to God, and now I'm trying to do things His way again."

Her hands covered her mouth. Whoa. Whoa, whoa, whoa. "You're a Christian?" she clarified.

His smile held awkwardness. "Yeah."

Her skin prickled at his confession. At the realization that her act of boldness in placing the Bible in the room had contributed to this man's renewal of faith. At the thought that maybe, just maybe, this man might be part of the answer to that prayer she'd prayed about her future. The backs of her eyes heated, and she ducked her head.

"And I figured that seeing it was Sunday, I should be in church." He glanced at her again. "I also figured you might know a good church for me to go to, but I didn't want you to think I was imposing again. I bet you do already, about all kinds of things."

Remorse grew. How awful that she'd resented this man, when God had simply had him on a path to finding Him?

"I'm so happy for you, Harrison. Really. And you know any church would be delighted to have you join with them. Some churches might find a Hollywood actor in their midst a little overwhelming, but it shouldn't be about that. It should be about finding a church community that encourages and supports you to grow in God."

Her words echoed in her mind. How often had she made it

about herself, rather than seeing things from the bigger perspective?

"Thanks." He swallowed. "I know I struggle with negativity sometimes, but I own my past behavior, and I want you to know I'm trying to change."

Was that a plea? It sure sounded like a plea for understanding. For acceptance. She glanced at him. This man was a brother in Christ. But more than that, she'd never had a right to hold offense due to anything he'd done, because as a Christian, she was supposed to let all offenses be placed at the foot of the cross. But she hadn't. Call it weariness or busyness or whatever, but she'd gotten way too good at nursing resentment and grudges and holding people's sins against them. He wasn't the real sinner here. She had been.

Regret squeezed her heart. *Lord, I'm sorry.*

He cleared his throat. "Anyway, I just wanted to say that I'm sorry, Cassie. For all the wrong things I've done." He held out his hand. "And I hope you'll forgive me."

She studied his hand, but this time she couldn't ignore it or make some careless comment. This moment held a weight, a weight that felt like it held seeds of the future. Would she forgive and let God have His way? There was only one answer.

"Of course. And," she swallowed. "I hope you'll forgive me too. I, um, haven't exactly been shining the light of Jesus either."

"Forgiven." His grip firmed as his smile lit his eyes.

Oh. Her heart fluttered, as she was again reminded why this man had been accorded heartthrob status on the show. When he smiled with his whole face like that, a girl could very easily get carried away and start believing he meant it for real. And while he might mean it in this moment, and want to have peace with her, she didn't dare for a second hope he wanted anything more. And even though there was now no longer the barrier of non-shared faith, she'd need to work extra hard now to tamp down any wandering thoughts that might beg to differ. As he'd made perfectly clear, her future was here. His wasn't.

She drew her hand away. Went to wipe it on her jeans then realized he might take that the wrong way. That wasn't kind. Even if it was more about her own preservation.

"Well, I'm glad we've got that cleared up."

"Me too." He smiled again, and again her heart begged to get carried off to fantasy land. But she wouldn't go there. She *wouldn't*, she told herself fiercely.

Because this man dealt with make-believe fiction, while she dealt with cold hard facts. And while God might hold their futures in His hand, she wasn't going to let her heart bob up and down like an air mattress on the creek, waiting, wondering, hoping for something that surely would not be. She'd have to trust God to have His way.

"I, uh, haven't really said any of that to anyone before. It's definitely not on my IMDB profile."

"You don't have to worry about me."

His eyebrows lifted. "You sure?"

She mimed zipping her lip and throwing away the key. "Mm-hm."

His lips tweaked wryly, and she was glad to get that much amusement from him.

"You're all right, Ms. James."

Her throat grew tight. Only all right? Maybe she wasn't as oblivious to him as she wanted to be, after all.

She pushed off the porch, dusting her hands on the back of her jeans. Stole a look at him as she repositioned her cowboy hat. "I don't think you know just how right I can be." She permitted a small curve of her mouth and pistol-pointed at him. "You better watch out. I'll be praying."

"Really?"

She dipped her chin, and secured her hat more firmly.

"Thanks."

Her lips lifted, and his did the same, and she was tempted to maintain the connection. But it wasn't wise. Would only end in heartbreak. So she muttered an excuse and walked away.

Harrison watched her stride away, her jeans hugging her like an ad for Levi's. He exhaled, glanced down at his scuffed boots. He really shouldn't be paying attention to things like that. Especially when it now felt like that by sharing his past she was now walking away with a tiny piece of his soul. And he hated the fact that she'd seen him so weak. He already knew himself to be so pitiful in comparison to her general awesomeness, that to expose himself to her pity made him feel even more like the dust under her boots.

He snuck another look at her. He'd seen how she'd wiped her hands of him. Literally. He'd savored her touch—heck, he wouldn't have said no to a hug, he'd been so desperate—but she obviously didn't want any part of that. Instead, she'd wiped away his touch like she couldn't wait to get rid of him. Just like she'd walked away as quick as she could after he'd poured out his heart to her. She didn't want him. And who could blame her? He'd revealed his brokenness and perfect her with her perfect family hadn't liked what she'd seen.

He reached into his pocket, pulled out his grandmother's cameo brooch, and traced the perfect lines on the woman's face.

THIRTEEN

She didn't know what to do. Harrison's salvation was an awesome thing, a miraculous thing, a wonderful answer to prayer, but what was she now supposed to do with this information?

She returned home and told her parents, who were both so overjoyed her mom insisted that Cassie invite him for a meal. But that sounded too much like a set up for a date, and because she was still unsure about so many things about him, she wasn't certain she could do that right now.

"Besides," she told her mom, "I don't have his number."

"But I do," her dad said.

"Why?"

Her dad shrugged. "Because I told him he could call me if he wanted to discuss some of those verses we talked about the other day."

Oh.

"Then you call him," Mom said.

Her dad did, but was met with a polite decline. Dad finished the call and studied Cassie. "He said he doesn't want to come and bother you by being in your space."

Way to go by laying on the guilt.

"He does have a point," Mom said. "This is Cassie's home, and while it's wonderful to encourage a young Christian in matters of the Lord, I can see the potential for complications if it happens here."

Mom sounded like she was trying to tiptoe through land-mines with that conversation. Exactly what had Harrison said to her parents on Friday night? Had he said something about her? Is that why her mother was being cagey?

Her mother looked at her. "Cassie, I know that I may have accused you of being lacking in the hospitality or grace depart-ment, but I understand now that this has not been easy. I'm sorry if I've done things that have made you feel hurt. That was never my intention."

"I know that, Mom. I do appreciate you saying it though. Because it hasn't been easy."

Her mom's eyes softened. "Why do you think that is?"

"Because I haven't really known what to do with these feelings."

"Feelings about Harrison?"

She nodded. "He told me before that he likes me, and I said that I couldn't go out with someone who wasn't a Christian, but now he is, I don't know what to do."

"It's early days," her mom cautioned. "Nobody is saying you have to go out with him, especially if you don't want to."

"But that's the thing," she whispered. "I think I do. He's a lot nicer than I first thought, and he's fun, and for some reason he seems to value me. But even that scares me because I can't see a future with a man who lives in Hollywood. How can that work when I live and work here?"

"But you don't have to live and work here forever."

"Mom, you know it's been my dream since I was a little girl to run this ranch one day."

"But dreams can change." Her mother smiled. "I used to dream of being an academic, like Hannah's mother, and then I met your father and visited Three Creek Ranch. I soon knew that I had a different call on my life."

Huh. "I never knew that."

"*As The Heart Draws* isn't just the pretty title of a book or a TV show, Cassie. God is in the business of drawing people to Himself, and He uses the Holy Spirit to touch people's hearts, in the hopes that they will find a relationship with Him."

Okay... "I know that. And we've seen that just now. But I'm already walking with God." Her lips twisted wryly. "Admittedly I haven't been walking too closely, but I'm trying to be better."

"But the Holy Spirit keeps prodding and pressing and speaking to people, not just to salvation, but to allow people to be shaped into God's purposes for their lives. Whether that means you change or God does something dramatic in a person's life and alters their careers, we just have to keep following those inklings when they come."

She nodded. She knew that too. Knew the implications of what happened when she didn't do that. Like that still small voice would end up speaking even more faintly.

CASSIE TUCKED her mother's words close to her heart as she went to work the next day. And the next. And the rest of the week. She was thankful that summer meant Three Creek Ranch's haying needed attention, and she could help her dad instead of possibly running into Harrison on the set. It gave her more time to figure out what to say.

She just hadn't expected her father to ask about her feelings for Harrison, something Dad had never done for any guy she'd liked before.

She'd admitted to feeling conflicted, and he nodded. "Even I can see he's got some charm, but you do need to be careful. He's a new Christian, and while I sense that these are questions that have been tugging at him for a long time, it's easy for some of those emotions to get mixed up with relationship stuff, and we don't want to confuse him."

"Which is why I'm very happy not to try to make anything happen."

"I think that's wise."

She kept praying for wisdom, and the thought crossed her mind to return to Franklin's apartment. But with her brother and Hannah returning from their honeymoon this week, her presence probably wouldn't be welcome. And part of her despised the idea of changing her routine just because a man was involved. Maybe Hannah's mom's feminist views had rubbed off on her more than she suspected, but it didn't seem the way a modern woman should live. Especially for someone who was going to try to keep her feelings for him tamped in the brotherly department. He was a brother in Christ now, after all.

Her phone buzzed in her back pocket. Mal. She called to her dad, "I need to take this call."

"Cassie? Thank you for coming by."

Cassie settled into the seat that Mal gestured to in the dining room. Mal had asked to see her without providing details, but the look on his face didn't suggest any trouble. "What can I help you with?"

"We wanted to run something by you, and you don't have to say yes, but it would be wonderful if you did."

"I'm happy to help if I can."

"We have a scene that we're shooting soon, and we just received word that Brenda—remember our stunt woman?—is sick and unable to join us in time."

"Oh, I didn't know. Poor thing."

He coughed. "Actually, I understand that she's not really sick. Apparently Harrison talked to her and convinced her to make a complaint about domestic violence."

Her breath hitched. "Poor Brenda." And good on Harrison. Although how had he recognized that?

"Yeah, we're doing what we can to support her. But in the meantime, we need someone to take her spot who can do it in a hurry. And, well, we've all seen your amazing riding skills, so we wondered if you might be interested."

"Me?" Was he serious? "I'm not a stunt woman."

"But you can ride a horse. And that's all we require. We just need a woman riding a horse along the ridge and she has an accident and she gets rescued by our hero."

Of course she did. She rolled her eyes internally. It was always the woman needing rescuing. Never the man.

Maybe something of that showed on her face because Mal's head tilted. "Is something wrong? If you're worried about what's involved we're only talking riding a horse, so there's no real risk of injury. Not for someone of your experience. You don't have to do it if you don't wish to. It just means that we'll need to reschedule how we do things."

"No, it's not that." She drew in a breath. "It's just the helpless female needing rescuing by a man that I'm not a fan of. It's certainly not been my experience." Try the other way around.

Mal's eyes widened like she was suddenly speaking Japanese.

She hurried to add, "I don't mean to sound disparaging, because I know people have different strengths and weaknesses. I just think it'd be good to see women having their strengths recognized too, that they'd be considered equal to a man and not feeble or weak."

His brow lowered, his gaze thoughtful. "I know you're tough, but I heard rumors from some of the cast that Harrison once saved you from a snake."

"It was non-venomous, so I didn't really need rescuing."

"Ah." He frowned, his fingers tapping the table between them. "Would you prefer not to work with Harrison, is that it?"

"No." The thought of potentially working with him gave shivers of both dread and anticipation. She hadn't seen him now in what felt like forever. How was he doing? Was he growing in faith? How had he known about Brenda's domestic strife? She forced herself to focus on Mal's question. "I guess I just feel that it'd be more interesting if the man and woman saved someone together. Or she saved him," she dared.

He chuckled. "Don't tell me you're wanting to write our scripts now?"

"No, of course not. But it would be nice to see women being presented in a way that's not reinforcing stereotypes of women being weak."

Mal frowned, and when he spoke his voice was stiff. "I didn't think our show did that."

She winced. She really needed to work on cultivating graciousness. "I'm sorry, Mal. I didn't mean to make it sound like that. You know I'm a big fan of this show." She gave an apologetic smile. "I guess I'm just a little amazed at being asked to do this."

"Well, never mind. I can see that you have strong opinions about this. We'll just re-organize our shooting schedule and not cause you to compromise your values."

Whoa. Someone was offended. "Mal, no, I'm happy to do it. I just meant—"

"I'm sorry for wasting your time today."

"But—"

"It's fine, Cassie. "

Her heart tensed as she exited the room. It clearly wasn't fine.

Harrison glanced around the dining area where an unscheduled production meeting had been called after the midday meal. Most of the senior cast and crew were there, along with one of the lead writers. Jerry was visiting the set again and seemed a nice enough guy. Ainsley had said Mal liked Jerry to touch base occasionally with the actors to get feedback on how things were going, especially given the latest ratings had just come in. Harrison had also heard rumors there might be questions about the future of some of the actors. Not himself obviously, because his work hadn't screened yet, but some of those others who might not be gelling with the audience in the way the producers wanted. So this meeting could prove quite interesting.

Mal got up and knocked on the table several times to get people's attention. "Thank you everyone for gathering together at short notice. I figured it's easier to explain now that we're all together. You all know Jerry, right?"

Harrison nodded as Mal looked his way.

"As you're probably aware, the recent ratings for our final season have just come in and Jerry is here to help us as we try to iron out a few issues."

The tension around the room ratcheted up. Nobody wanted to think a cast member's role was on the line, but such was the nature of the business. And it was a business, as a show's popularity had a direct impact on the kinds of sponsors and advertising dollars involved. Anything that potentially affected a show's ability to bring in the dollars and affect the network's bottom line would be cut. It was why actors risked losing their roles if they were perceived as immoral. A wholesome family-friendly show like *As The Heart Draws* couldn't risk a whiff of suspicion and lose popularity and ratings. Similarly, if the audience didn't connect with a character, they might end up being sent away, or worse, killed off, never to return. His lips twisted. There was no way to come back from a grave—although it had happened a few times in various daytime soaps.

"In addition to that, we have a bit of a snafu with one of our scenes, and now it looks like we're going to have to reschedule things until we have a stunt woman in place who can do it." He glanced around the table. "I presume you all know about Brenda?"

Harrison's heart knotted, and he shot up a quick prayer for her.

"We like to consider ourselves a family here, so it hurts to think Brenda was dealing with this on her own." Mal glanced at him. "Until Harrison drew this to our attention."

He shrugged. "My dad wasn't a nice man, so I've come to recognize some of the signs."

Mal nodded. "So, with Brenda out, and with our strict time frames and no substitute available until the end of next week, we'll have to reconfigure things."

Ainsley raised her hand. "I thought you were going to ask Cassie to do it."

Harrison's heart thudded. He had?

"I did, but she indicated she would prefer to not be the helpless female in this scenario and declined."

Hope deflated.

"Well, I don't blame her," Dana murmured. "Why does it always have to be the man who saves the day?"

"Exactly." Ainsley offered Jerry a sweet smile. "No offense, Jerry, but I'm kind of tired of Abigail looking like she needs help from a big strong man all the time." She gestured toward outside. "The west wasn't won by weak women. Women have always had to be strong to build families and communities and endure the challenges of life and these conditions."

"Amen," Dana said.

Huh. Good on them for standing up for their opinions.

"But this is what our viewers want." Mal glanced at Jerry who nodded.

"Is it though?" Ainsley folded her arms.

Huh. She sure was going in strong today. But then, as the main character around whom the others revolved, she was least likely to lose a role from butting heads with the showrunner. Ainsley *was* the heart that drew the most fans. Viewers loved her. Replacing her meant guaranteed audience mutiny and cellar-dwelling ratings.

"Yes, Ainsley," Mal resumed. "The polls show that our audience wants traditional values reinforced, which means how men and women are portrayed."

"We certainly don't think men are superior to women," Jerry added.

Ainsley lifted her chin. "I've played this role for the past four years, and in that time Abigail has been rescued from a coal mine, a flood, a fire, and a bear." She ticked off her fingers. "Every single time it's been Tanner's Mountie character who saved her. I understand the need for dramatic moments to build romantic tension, but I feel like if she was brave enough to come west to teach school by herself, then the audience wants to see that fearlessness again, and not see her perpetually as a weak woman. What kind of message does that send to the girls watching our show?"

Jerry's mouth tightened. "We need our Mounties to appear strong."

"And they can, but there are many different kinds of strength. Relationships should be an equal partnership. It doesn't always have to be at the sake of saving the woman."

"Are you saying you want Abigail to be in this scene, and she saves Harrison's character?" Mal asked.

"No. But I do think we need some strong females shown on screen, which is why I suggested Cassie. She's one of the toughest women I know—"

Yes, she was. Strong, capable, loyal, fierce but in a good way.

"—so I can't blame her for declining. But she might want to be part of things if it got changed. So is there any way to rework the scene?" Ainsley caught Harrison's eye, made a gesture, as if wanting him to contribute.

He'd read the scene, knew his character was supposed to save a woman on a runaway horse. And while he much preferred the idea of working with Cassie instead of Brenda, he didn't blame her for wanting out of a scene that had been portrayed on TV a million times before. He could see Ainsley's point.

Harrison cleared his throat. "I agree that Cassie is strong, and I don't mind admitting that I've been on the receiving end of her toughness. I think it'd be good to see that portrayed."

Mal sighed. "I'm afraid we'll just need to reschedule—"

"What about if she rescues him from the runaway horse?" Harrison interrupted.

Mal's brow lowered. "Nathaniel is a Mountie. He already knows how to control his horse so it wouldn't run away."

"But say it gets spooked. By a..."

"A snake," Ainsley supplied.

He half-smiled at her. He'd recently shared his new commitment with her and she'd hugged him, declaring she was thrilled. It wouldn't surprise him if she thought this now meant a green light as far as him seeking a relationship with Cassie. Maybe that was partly why she was gunning for this so hard.

"So she's rescuing him?" Mal frowned.

"No, that doesn't work," Jerry said. "She can't just save him then disappear. She would then have to become a continuing character and we're just talking about a cameo. Someone who's there and then gone and doesn't return."

Probably like how Cassie regarded him. Was that why she didn't want to get involved with him? He hadn't seen her since that Sunday evening, and it had now been eight days. Yes, he was counting. *Lord, could you please make a way?*

"You could always bump up her role and make it a recurring character?" Ainsley suggested, with a wink at Harrison.

"I don't think that's what we are going to do," Mal said firmly.

It was testament to the working relationships on *As The Heart Draws* that Mal hadn't shut this down already. Harrison had worked on many shows where the writers were basically gods, and the actors had no say in what their character did at all. He liked the collaborative approach here, although from the way Mal and Jerry were eyeing her, it'd be interesting to see what this might mean for Ainsley's future on the show.

"What if it's a double save," he suggested. "Like, his horse gets spooked by a snake so she saves him from a runaway horse, and then he saves her because she's bitten by the snake."

"How many snakes are we gonna have on this show?" Jerry asked, rolling his eyes.

"It doesn't have to be snakes. It could be a bear," Dustin said.

"Hmm. It *could* be a bear..." Mal tapped his chin. "But then we'd need to hire a bear, and they're expensive, and as Ainsley mentioned, Abigail has already had a bear encounter. So no, I really think—"

"What if it's a near drowning?" Dana suggested. "You could have him stop the horse but they end up in deep water, and he gets injured by a log and she helps him stay afloat."

"That sounds more believable." Ainsley nodded.

"And he still gets to be a hero, doing Mountie things," Harrison added.

"But doesn't that set her up as a heroine?" Mal said. "Viewers would be expecting to see her again."

"So maybe they do, in a recurring role. Or..." Ainsley straightened. "She could be someone from his past, and become the conflict between Abigail and Nathaniel because he's now got divided loyalties, and that continues through the season."

"But that would mean a far bigger role for Cassie."

"Well, it's not as if she has far to come to be on set."

"But she's not a trained actor. You don't even know if she'd want to do this."

"I can talk to her, and talk to my agent about her if necessary. And even if it's just this scene that she does as a stand-in for Brenda, and you introduce a new character, I think a scenario like that would help add some extra tension that helps drive the series."

"Hmm." Mal glanced at Jerry.

Jerry glanced at the ceiling, his brow furrowed, so you could almost see the wheels turning.

"I don't mind the idea of a runaway horse and a river," Mal said. "But we'd need a nearby river."

"There's a creek not too far from here," Harrison said. And he guessed the James family would be happy if it was used. "It has good access for vehicles, and some deeper water parts that might be good for filming."

"And you know this how?" Mal asked.

"Um, it might've got mentioned on the day I had a certain encounter with a reptile."

"I'm not going anywhere near a snake." Dana shuddered.

"But you wouldn't need to," Ainsley pointed out. "It'd only be Harrison and Cassie in this scene."

Mal nodded. "Let me think on this." He glanced at Harrison. "Would you be willing to act in water?"

It's what his signature on a contract said. And if it meant an excuse to be near Cassie again, then, "Absolutely."

One hundred percent.

And perhaps this was an answer to prayer.

FOURTEEN

Cassie herded the steers into the corral and shut them up, ready for loading to market. Her phone buzzed in her pocket. She pulled it out, checked the number. Why was Ainsley calling her?

"Hello?"

"Oh, Cassie. Have you got a few minutes?"

"Uh, sure." She moved away from the noise and leaned against the wooden barn. "What can I do for you?"

"See, that's exactly it." Ainsley sighed. "I might've got myself into a little bit of hot water and I'd really appreciate it if you could help me out."

Ainsley? The golden child of *As The Heart Draws* in hot water? "What have you done?"

"I might've got into an argument with Mal and Jerry, the lead writer. We had a meeting on set today."

Cassie's brows rose. "And you want me to help how?"

"Look, you probably know by now that I'm the one who recommended that you could be the substitute stunt rider in an upcoming scene."

"I'd wondered."

"The thing is, at our meeting today some of us discussed how bad it looks for the show to constantly reinforce women as being inferior to men and needing to be rescued by them all the time, which is what you said, right?"

She winced. "Yes. And Mal wasn't too happy about that."

"Well, I don't know how happy he was about me saying it either. But I did, and Dana and Harrison agreed that it sends the wrong message, when men are always portrayed as the heroes."

Her pulse glitched. "Harrison said that?"

"He did." Ainsley giggled. "He might've also mentioned how a certain cowgirl rescued him, but don't tell him I said that."

Cassie swatted at a fly, smiling. He'd said that about her?

"He also shared that he got saved recently. Not at the meeting, just privately to me, but isn't that awesome? I'm so excited for him! I've sent him a link to Lincoln Cash's new group for Holly-wood-based believers, and he's told me he has already reached out and attended his first Bible study."

Her throat was tight. "He has?"

"It helps when it's online."

"I'm so glad." It sounded like he really was growing in the things of God.

"Me too. He really is maturing, and we're praying together and everything."

Jealousy bit. But how could she complain when she'd basically ignored him? She couldn't blame him for finding spiritual encouragement where he could. She wondered if her father had been in touch with him.

"Anyway, back to the point, which is that I think you may get a phone call from Mal asking if you'd reconsider the role. I'm pretty sure he now wants to change it, and you may find that it ends up being a little bit bigger than what was originally proposed."

"What do you mean?"

"Look, I'm not privy to all of what Mal and Jerry have planned, but I hope that you will consider it."

"But I'm not an actor. Wouldn't I need to have an agent and union membership and all that kind of thing?"

"I can talk to Rosie, my agent, and I'm sure we can sort all of that out. The more important question is, would you like to do it?"

Her hat tilted forward as she considered. Sure she could keep doing what she'd always done, but Poppy was right. Opportunities passed. They didn't pause. And depending on what it was that Mal suggested, this might be an opportunity she didn't want passing her by.

Cassie's phone buzzed with another notification. She glanced at the screen. Her heart tensed. "It's Mal."

"Then take it, and let me know what you decide."

"Will do. Thanks. And bye." She switched calls. "Hi Mal."

"Cassie, have I caught you at a bad time?"

"Nope. I'm all yours. Shoot."

He chuckled. "You really are a cowgirl, aren't you?"

She watched a tumbleweed roll past. Darn tootin'.

"Look, I'm gonna cut to the chase. It's about that role I mentioned to you before. You'll be pleased to know that we've tweaked a number of aspects of that scene, and I'd like you to think about whether it's something you might like to do after all."

"In what ways has it changed?"

"We seem to have a number of people who agree with you that women in the show have not always been represented in the way that most would prefer. The suggestion was made that it could be a mutual rescuing situation where she helps him and he helps her."

"So she's not a helpless female?"

"No. I didn't personally feel that was what would be portrayed, but some of the other cast members disagreed. And we've listened to their concerns."

"What would I have to do?"

He explained, and she nodded, and they talked logistics, like actor's membership and scripts. Her words would be few, and she'd be forced to work with Harrison, just like Mal had mentioned before.

Her heart skittered. Work with Harrison. Him rescuing her, she helping him. Equal. Partners. Together. She shivered.

"So what I want to know is whether this is something that you feel like you could do."

Riding a horse was something she could do. Pretending to get in trouble in a creek was something she could do. Being in such close proximity to Harrison without it affecting her? That was trickier.

"Cassie? You still there?"

"I'm interested," she said cautiously. "But I need to check with a few people and see if I can make this work."

"I understand. I know this is a lot to consider, especially with all your work at the ranch."

Yeah, talking to her dad about ranch work wasn't who she meant. "How soon do you need to know?"

"By five today?"

She inhaled sharply. "Okay, I'll do my best."

It looked like she'd be talking to Harrison at last.

HARRISON PLACED his head in his hands as he studied his script. The afternoon's shooting was scheduled soon, and would involve his encounter with Ainsley outside the general store on Main Street. This type of scene made him glad he was staying here, with a simple walk into town rather than a hike over the hill. It looked straightforward enough, he had five lines, she had six, the exchange a simple way of keeping the potential for a relationship between Abigail and Nathaniel alive. *As The Heart Draws* had multiple storylines to give viewers several hooks to stay engaged, but the biggest draw was always who Abigail was romantically involved with.

He knew who he would like to be romantically involved with,

and it wasn't Abigail or Ainsley. But she hadn't spoken to him since that last Sunday. And while he was trying to find comfort in his new relationship with God, he felt a degree of anxiety about this strain with her.

What could he do to prove that he had changed? Ainsley said it would just take time. Lincoln Cash, in his Bible study, had said the same. People needed to see that Harrison had changed. Which meant things like forgiveness and repairing relationships and all kinds of things to show he wasn't the same man as before. But unless he talked with her, she'd never know. Unless she'd talked with her father and Derek mentioned something.

Harrison hadn't wanted to bother Derek too much, but the man had been persistent, and had contacted him several times, checking up to make sure Harrison was reading his Bible, connecting with Christians. He was, and each day he read the Bible he was sinking into deeper wonder about the promises of God. God, his Heavenly Father, who promised to never leave or forsake him. What a contrast to his own father who, when Harrison had tried to reach out last weekend, had ignored his call, and hadn't even replied to his text. He knew his dad had seen it too, because it had been marked as *Read*. His heart panged, but he'd also found that verse that said as far as it depended on him to live at peace with others, so he was leaving his dad up to God. Heaven knew that his dad needed God too. Which was an excellent reminder...

"Hey God," he closed his eyes. "I know that I'm new at all this stuff, but I want to trust You for my dad's salvation. I know I'm a long way short of perfect, but that's okay because You're perfect. And if You can raise the dead, and if You can change my heart, then You can change his too." His eyes watered. "And I wanted to say thank You for my salvation. Thank You for giving me a new start. And I'd really like it if You could somehow help Cassie see that I'm not the same man I used to be. And wherever she is today, please bless her. And bless my dad. And bless Derek and Leonie. And Ainsley. And Cassie. Amen."

Cassie.

He drew out the brooch that his grandmother had given him. Studied the profile, the one so similar to that photo of Cassie from the wedding. With her hair all fancy, it could be the same person, the same graceful line of neck, jaw and nose. She might be tough, but there was a gracefulness she possessed too. She wasn't hard, not like some women he'd met. And the fact God was working in her heart proved it even more so.

"Lord, bless her."

His phone buzzed on the table next to his script. A reminder. Thirty minutes until show time. He needed to get into his Mountie uniform then get ready for hair and makeup, something that could be done on site because it just involved a quick brush and a minute applying what he called face paint. He thanked God for the hundredth time he wasn't a woman and had to spend hours in a chair. His lips twisted. Just another discrepancy between men and women on this show.

A knock came at the door. Maxine, most likely, here to remind him.

He opened it, then nearly fell backwards. "Um, hi."

Cassie's smile was tentative. "Hi. I'm really sorry for intruding like this, but I've wanted to talk to you about something."

"Um." He winced. "I hate to say this, but I'm kind of in a rush. I start shooting at two."

Her nose wrinkled. "How long will that go for?"

"A few hours, probably."

"Oh." Her face fell. "Okay."

It clearly wasn't okay. "We can talk after. I'd love to talk to you too. And I promise, I won't make it weird or anything—or at least I'll try not to make it weird, but with me there are no guarantees."

She half-smiled. "Okay. I need to give Mal my answer by five. I just wanted to talk to you about it first."

"Your answer?" His heart thumped. "Is this about the role? Are you gonna do it?"

"I thought it sounded interesting, although I was sad to hear about Brenda." She eyed him. "Mal mentioned that you encouraged her to report the domestic violence."

He nodded. "My dad used to beat my mom. And me."

Her breath hitched. "Oh, Harrison."

He half-shrugged. "That's why I couldn't watch another woman face that. Not like my mom did." He shook his head. "I should've stood up for her more."

"But you must've been young. Just a boy."

"It doesn't change the fact that I still regret not standing up for her more."

Her eyes were soft, her compassion palpable. "I'm so sorry this happened."

His lips tweaked. "But I don't want to live in the past. I've learned a lot in recent days about letting go and letting God have His way."

"Me too," she murmured, gaze still fixed on him.

His heart flickered. Did that mean she might see him as part of her future? Why else would she have asked that question before?

He cleared his throat. "So, does this mean you'll consider the role?"

Her smile twisted. "I have to confess that I've never once dreamed of being an actor, and I'm pretty sure that I couldn't act my way out of a paper bag, but it does sound like an interesting opportunity."

"Wait—did you just say you've never once dreamed about being an actor?"

"I used to dream about being Annie Oakley," she said with a shy-looking smile.

He laughed. "Of course you did."

"Whereas I bet you dream about getting Golden Globes, huh?"

They might not have known each other too long, but she knew him so well. "Maybe."

He beckoned her inside, but she shook her head. Then he realized what it would look like if she was inside his room should Maxine or someone else come along. Wise woman. "So what was it you wanted to ask?"

"Didn't you need to get ready or something?"

"This sounds more important." His heart swelled. "You are more important."

Her lips flickered, like she wasn't sure whether to believe him. "Well, that's the thing. Could we—you and me—can we do this?"

"Act together? Or...?" He arched a brow.

She blushed.

Aw, who would've thought the cowgirl knew how to blush. He liked it. A lot. And he liked the fact she was affected by him. Surely that meant there was hope.

"Act together."

"Well of course we can."

"But without it getting weird."

"Like I said earlier, weird is part of my DNA, so I can't promise no weirdness."

"No, I mean you and me, and, um..."

He leaned against the doorframe. Maybe it was mean to be loving the awkwardness she was displaying, but the fact she couldn't articulate the attraction that throbbed between them had to mean she felt something, right? "And um...?"

She exhaled. "You're enjoying this, aren't you?"

"Maybe a little bit."

"Fine. Okay, I'll spell it out in one syllable words. Do you still like me?"

"Darn straight."

"I mean as, um, more than a friend?"

His heart picked up speed. "One hundred percent."

"Will you make it weird if we have to be together and um, touch, and so on if I was to take the role?"

He avoided pointing out that "together" was three syllables, his amusement dying at the pleading look she gave him. He desperately wanted to hold her hand, but knew this wasn't the time. He'd let her take the lead and make the decisions on anything like that. "If you take the role I promise you that I will be a perfect gentleman. I won't get into your space, I won't have any expectations. I care about you, Cassie. I really care about you."

Her breath hitched. "But why?"

His heart panged, her question revealing some of her own insecurities. Who had dared hurt this woman to make her question her self-worth? "You are unlike any woman I've met. You're so strong and that makes me want to be a better man. Yet you also have this sweet softness, and godly values that reminds me of my grandma, and she was the best woman I've ever known."

Her expression that had owned skepticism at being compared to his grandmother melded into surprise then a tentative smile.

Phew. Note to self: do not tell the woman you're hoping to impress that she's like your grandmother.

"Anyway," he continued, "I like you, but God is teaching me to be patient, not to want my own way. I have to admit that's really hard because I have been pretty selfish for the past thirty years."

"I'm not great at being unselfish either," she admitted. "But I'm trying to do better."

"Thank God for the Holy Spirit helping us, huh?"

Her eyes widened. "You really have changed."

Pride pinged inside his chest. Well, except pride was a sin, he knew that now. He'd go with gladness instead. *Thanks God that she noticed.* "I'm still a work in progress."

Her mouth twisted wryly. "Aren't we all?"

"I'm just so grateful for people like your dad and Lincoln Cash and Ainsley, who have taken time to help me grow and understand."

She wet her lip, and he had to breathe out against the desire to rush and kiss her. He wouldn't. Not now. He was a changed man.

Cassie steadily gazed at him, and he at her, as the connection between them flared. He could study this woman all day. She fascinated him with her mix of strength and vulnerability, raw beauty, smarts and sass. Her smile grew, and it was getting increasingly hard to tamp down his desire for more.

He exhaled. "I hope that answers your question, Miss Cassie."

She nodded. "It does."

"But I have one for you."

Her head tilted. "What is it?"

"If you should happen to, I don't know, decide that you like me, then I'm totally okay with you letting me know."

"That's not a question."

"You're right. But I mean it just the same."

Her gaze pinned him, the air trembling with emotion, promise and potential. "You like me." She said it almost as a question, like she couldn't believe what he'd said before.

Clearly he needed to make things more plain. "I do." He held his hands up, an act of surrender. "And yes, I want to get to know you more, with a view to having a relationship with you that lasts, that isn't a summer fling. And I know the only way I can really do that is by letting you take the lead. So I will be right here waiting for you to let me know when that right moment will be, for however long that might take."

"Th-thank you."

"I mean it. I'm here for you, and want to explore what having a relationship might look like. And I know that could get tricky, with you here, and me wherever work takes me, but I don't think God brings people into each other's lives without it meaning something. I like you, and I'm really hoping this conversation means that you like me."

Her smile widened and she dipped her chin.

He internally fist-pumped. Then smiled. "But why?" he gently teased, returning her question from before.

Her chuckle was like a warm hug on a cold day. He needed more of that in his life.

"Because you care about people, and you're willing to be brave and face your fears, and even be brave enough to admit your mistakes. That takes real courage."

He might've been on movie screens around the world, but he'd never felt quite so seen. He swallowed a lump of emotion.

"And you're kind of fun to hang out with," Cassie continued.

"Only kind of?"

She gave another burble of laughter. "And there I was thinking you maybe weren't so arrogant after all."

He grinned. He'd missed this banter, the snap and crackle of a witty woman. But this time there was no animosity behind it. Instead, he sensed something good. Something God-honoring. Something that may well have enough substance for a future. "So let's commit all this to God, and see where He takes us."

She swallowed, her gaze steady, sure. "Okay."

"Okay?"

She nodded. "So go on then. Pray."

Wow. Good thing he'd had some practice praying aloud with others recently. He wondered if he should hold her hand or whether that was simply temptation calling him, then figured God could probably hear him even if he didn't. He closed his eyes though. She was too distracting. "Hey Lord, we give this, uh, friendship to You, and ask You to have Your way in our hearts. If this is of You, then please make a way. If it's not, thank You that You know what You're doing and help us to trust You. Amen."

He opened his eyes, saw Cassie wipe away a tear, her smile tremulous. Then saw Maxine standing behind her, her mouth agape.

"That was beautiful," Cassie said. "Thanks."

Maxine cleared her throat, causing Cassie to jump. "Um, I don't know what I've just interrupted here, but Harrison, they're asking for you on set."

Ouch. "Sorry, Cassie, I better hustle ."

"Thanks for talking."

"You're welcome."

Her smile filled his heart, her promise buoying him as he scrambled into his costume, hastened to set, and listened to Mal's complaint about being kept waiting.

But he didn't mind. Cassie liked him. She really liked him.

God was so good and was working things out.

FIFTEEN

"Now, don't breathe in too tight," Glenda said to Cassie. "You still need to be able to fit it when you're actually moving."

Why had she agreed to doing this? Because opportunities for a cameo for a cowgirl didn't come every day. As Poppy liked to say, opportunities passed, they didn't pause. So it was either help out and try this today, or forever wonder what if.

Which was why she was standing here, in the costume fitting department, trying to fit into some of those clothes that she'd always hung up in the prop barn, but had never thought that she might actually wear herself. Although the way she was going, there was a danger she wouldn't even be able to fit into this. Proof that perhaps she'd indulged in a little too much honeycomb ice cream of late.

She soon found a way of adjusting the skirt and corset, so it didn't bite her ribs too hard. And it had to be said the corset gave her a figure she hadn't owned since her bridesmaid dress. She wondered what Harrison would say when he saw her.

Her stomach swirled in anticipation. She hadn't seen him since that last encounter, with ranch work keeping her busy. But she soon would be in close proximity with Harrison, and after that last encounter when he'd prayed—he'd *prayed!*—she now sensed that this time together with him today—and potentially in the future—could really be okay. She could do this. They were both Christians. And adults. And seeing he still liked her—which still felt impossible but he'd said it, so he probably meant it—then the cameras would ensure no funny business could occur. At least until the cameras stopped, and she'd finally get the chance to find out whether he meant what he'd said before, or if he'd just been acting.

After she'd agreed, and Ainsley had got her agent to sign her up, and she'd signed a million forms and waivers, Mal had discussed the role in more detail.

Apparently, all she had to do was ride her horse—she even got to use Ginger—and creative license would show her thrown into a river, which was actually the creek of infamy from several weeks ago. Oh, she hoped there'd be no snakes involved today.

A short time later, she was in hair and makeup. It felt strange to be wearing this much make up again for the second time in four weeks, but she did have to admit the end result looked pretty nice, especially the fat curls in her hair. And when she finally exited the make-up trailer, she was met with a wolf whistle.

"Cassie? Hello, is that Cassie?" Ainsley grinned. "Girl, you look good."

"Like I'm ready to stop a runaway horse?"

"Like you're ready to give a certain Mountie a heart attack."

Her cheeks heated, and she picked up the edge of her skirt like Ainsley did. Look at her, getting lessons at her age on how to act like a lady.

Then when she moved to the corral where Ginger was, she saw Harrison, who was stroking and talking to his horse. Dressed in the red and navy of a Mountie, he was everything handsome and honorable and heroic. Her heart fluttered. And now he was a Christian, Harrison was everything that a hero should be.

He turned and spotted her, his eyes widening, and he looked her up and down. Then gulped. Audibly.

Ainsley snickered, Ted chuckled, and Cassie's cheeks grew hotter.

"Are you sure you're gonna manage in this scene?" Ainsley teased him.

"If you need a replacement for Cassie, you can always use me," Annie called. "I'd be happy to be rescued by Sweet Cheeks there any time he likes."

Her husband guffawed. "I don't know that the feeling would be mutual, honey."

Harrison laughed but didn't deny it, his gaze still fixed on Cassie.

Okay, from that look of intensity, he did indeed still like her. She shivered, her fingers plucking at the lacework on her puffed sleeve.

"Ah, good. You're both here." Mal gestured them over to the vehicle that would take them to the creek. "Walk with me while I explain a few last-minute things."

"Have fun today," Ainsley murmured. "I'll be praying for you."

"Thanks. I'll need it."

"You'll be fine," Ainsley assured.

Harrison patted his horse again and joined her at Mal's truck.

"So, I understand that you know the country here better than anyone, Cassie. But for this, we need your hair and make-up to stay in place as much as possible so it looks as it should on camera. So we're gonna drive you over and that way you won't get too messed up before we're ready to shoot."

"Fair enough."

"Harrison, it'll be the same for you. We need our hero to stay handsome for as long as possible."

Cassie snuck a look at him. Sure enough, his gaze was fixed on her still, his smile looking like it was branded on.

"Any questions?" Mal asked.

She shook her head.

"No, sir," Harrison said.

"Good. Well, let's get going."

Harrison opened the car's back door to her, murmuring "You look beautiful."

She smiled, and slid in, then he closed the door and hurried to the other side and got in the back too. Mal sat in front next to the driver, checking over notes as the driver took them closer to the creek, the site of today's drama. She glanced down at Harrison's hand, resting near hers, and wondered if he knew how nervous she was. And it wasn't just nerves about a role she'd never done before, but also about how to manage being in such close proximity to him. Because while this was acting, there was also a degree of realness in wanting this man to actually be her hero.

Her finger inched closer, Harrison looked down from where he was reading his script, then looked at her. Again, she sank into the depths of his gaze, wondering if he remembered what he'd said last time, about letting her lead the way. Well, she wasn't as forward as some. Putting her hand next to his was about as forward as she could be. Her finger fluttered, grazing his, and a frisson of anticipation shivered between them as he cocked a brow in a silent question.

She smiled a *yes*, he nodded, and his fingers wrapped around hers. Her breath hitched, and she glanced down. This time she didn't pull away. This time she was glad to have him near. His hand held strength, and surety, and promise.

Mal glanced back, his eyebrows lifting as he saw their joined hands. He cleared his throat.

She tugged her hand away, but Harrison retained it.

"Hmm. I'd heard some rumors, but I was never really sure. Is there something I should know?" Mal asked.

"Not yet, sir. But I hope there might be soon." Harrison glanced at her. "It depends on what Miss Cassie here says."

Miss Cassie couldn't speak to save herself, her throat was so dry. She leaned forward, snagged her water bottle from its holder in the door, and sucked down blessedly cool water.

"Well, I can see that Nathaniel will definitely have his work cut out in terms of providing believable chemistry with Abigail, so don't go getting too hot and heavy today you two."

Now her cheeks were blazing.

Harrison gently squeezed her hand, and smiled. "Last I remember that creek wasn't too hot, so you won't need to worry."

How weird that she could wrangle a baby bull to the ground but this man made her feel weaker than one of Miranda's newborn kittens. She could suddenly understand why romance fiction had so many women swooning. She'd always wondered what made a hero swoony. Now she knew. She was glad she was sitting down because her knees felt weak.

They arrived at the creek, and it wasn't long before the horse trailers arrived with Ginger and Harrison's horse. She'd been told there would be some shots taken of her riding along the ridge, and she was happy enough to start her acting career with that.

"Break a leg," Harrison murmured, pressing his hands together in a praying motion, before she was whisked away by Mal.

"Okay, Cassie. You understand where to go?"

She nodded. They'd run through this a few times.

"So on my count, I want you to ride along the ridge. We'll have someone in place to let you know when the scene is done."

She mounted Ginger, and patted her mane, praying the mare wouldn't feel Cassie's nerves. Thank goodness her role meant she didn't need to ride side-saddle. Her skirts were long enough and the scene would be shot from a distance, so viewers wouldn't be able to tell the difference. The backstory was that she was alone, the lone survivor of an outbreak or disease at a farming community not too far away, and was sick and looking for help. When Mal had explained that, she didn't mind looking helpless. It made sense if one was sick, then one would struggle to fend for oneself. Then a snake would spook Harrison's horse, and she would try to save him. Finally, they'd both end up in the river where he'd help her, and they'd realize they knew each other from before.

"Ready?"

She sucked in a breath. Nodded.

"Go!"

She nudged Ginger, and they soon were galloping along the ridge, the wind blowing her beautifully curled ringlets awry. She glanced back, as Mal required, then bent down slightly, to suggest speed. Different poses would be spliced together to show from Harrison's perspective from where he was positioned closer to the creek.

She peeked down the gully, saw his red coat down near the water, and memories surged of that day when he really had tried to be the hero. Fresh appreciation rose for him and for his forbearance towards her. She couldn't wait for the chance when they could be alone and she could finally show him her gratitude.

An assistant waved a "cut" and she drew Ginger to a trot, then moved back to where Mal waited, studying the computer as the camera footage played back.

"That looks really good." He glanced at her. "Maybe you'll be a one cut wonder."

"I'm happy if you are."

"Then let's move on." Mal gave orders to set up for the next shot, when Ginger would be running toward the creek. This was when she had to act more, as her face would be seen. Normally a stunt person was doubling for a lead role, but because her role was new, it meant she would be seen more closely. She shivered. But not as close as the upcoming scene in the water.

"You doing okay?" Mal asked.

"Yep. I just hope we can get this done so I can do the water scenes while it's still warm."

"Good point. Alrighty people, let's go," Mal ordered.

She needed several takes for this scene—apparently her face hadn't appeared quite scared enough. Her efforts to look afraid, gave her new appreciation for what people like Ainsley and Harrison had to do. Act with your face? Who knew?

This was soon accomplished, then they stopped for a break. She moved to where Harrison was sitting, running his lines. He had multiple lines to rehearse, and she had two: "Help me!" and "Here." It shouldn't be too hard to remember that.

Harrison looked up, then immediately put his script down and stood. "How are you doing?" His face held concern. "Are you doing okay?"

"It's fine. I'm fine. I just can't believe how much sitting around there is."

He chuckled. "Don't say that too loudly. Mal likes to think he's pretty focused and I have to say this is one of the more efficient productions I've worked on. But Mal is used to shooting with this crew and cast, so they don't need as much instruction as some, or so Ainsley says."

"She seems to be a fan of yours."

"And of you. You should've heard her declaring that she wanted this scenario to be about equal opportunity, so who knows what that means for future seasons? Maybe one day we'll have a female sheriff."

She laughed. "Like that wouldn't be historically inaccurate at all."

He grinned. "Unlike that Jane Austen movie you were watching."

"You know it?"

"I've heard about it, and I could tell from what little bit I saw that Jane would be rolling in her grave."

"I'd still like to see the rest of it one day."

He eyed her. "Maybe we could watch it together."

She swallowed. "Like on a date?"

He nodded. "Or it could be just friends together. Up to you."

A man who let her call the shots like this? He could definitely be called date-worthy.

"Well, if you do decide to watch it, make sure you follow it with a more faithful adaptation. I'm a big fan of the Romola Garai *Emma* miniseries."

"Because?"

"Because she gives the character of Emma a degree of humanity, so we feel for her, rather than some adaptations that make it hard to care for a character who can come across as a little arrogant."

She studied him, wondering if he referred to more than just the character of Emma in that statement. "Sometimes the viewer needs a little longer to truly understand a person."

"And sometimes a man can take a person's measure at a glance." He smiled.

Her heart fluttered. Did he mean to suggest he had fallen for her quickly? "That certainly wasn't true in our case."

"Maybe two glances for me, then."

She chuckled. "Come on. At least five."

"Hey, I just didn't know who I was dealing with." His head tilted. "Does this mean what I hope it means?"

"It depends on what you hope it means," she said, channeling her inner Ainsley coyness.

His smile broadened. "It means I really hope that you're not wishing me to leave, because I really would like the chance to take you out for dinner."

Her stomach swooped. "Well, a girl has to eat, I suppose."

His eyes lit. "So that's a yes? Tonight?"

"Maybe."

"Aw, please don't *maybe* me, Cassie. You know I've been wanting this for ages—"

"Have you two finished?" Mal called. "Come on. Let's get this scene done."

She rose, her makeup was adjusted, but there was little point in too much. Most of this scene would be focused on Harrison. Harrison—who she'd be having dinner with tonight!

Due to the cold temperatures of the water she was instructed to pull on surf leggings which fit nicely under her skirt. She hoped they could do this quickly.

"Ready?" Harrison asked her.

"As I'll ever be." *Thank You God for keeping us safe.*

She followed Mal to where she was supposed to be, and held

Ginger's reins. Thanks to the magic of motion picture the scene of her cantering to the water's edge would be interspersed with Harrison on Buddy. She would catch up to him and then they would have a series of shots taken while she was not riding but it would be made to look like she was. She'd grab Buddy's reins and slow the horse, then Harrison would fall onto a crash mat. Then there'd be another shot of him falling into the water.

The next two hours were busy, a chaotic scramble of shots. Harrison was dumped into the creek then dried off, dunked then dried off, until Mal pronounced himself satisfied.

Then it was her turn. The safety advisor had instructed where they were to stand, and what they would do. She would wade into the water, find the underwater safety hand rail that they'd stand behind, and they'd "struggle" to swim while cameras from all different angles filmed.

"We'll keep rolling, because we don't want to have to put you through this too many times, and we can splice and dice as necessary if we have footage from all kinds of angles to work with."

It felt funny to think that this pool in the creek where she had gone swimming all her life would now be considered a hazard on the screens of millions around the world, but such was the nature of storytelling.

She followed Mal's cues, and winced as directed as the cold water seeped through her clothes. There was a world of difference between swimming here on a hot day in her swimsuit and being layered in clothes. It was so heavy. And all the physical falling down before meant it was already hard to breathe. She was waist deep, searching for the makeshift rail as their safety protocols warranted.

"You okay?" Harrison murmured.

"Yeah. You?"

He grinned. "Yes."

"No smiling," Mal called. "This is serious. Now, remember, you need to look like you're in trouble."

"Oh, I am," Harrison murmured. "I'm standing next to her, and all I can think about is the last time we were here."

She bit back a smile.

"That's it, Cassie," Mal called. "Look like you're in pain."

"Are you in pain?" Harrison asked.

"No." Except, the weight of all her clothes was making it hard to stand steady on the rocks below. She could suddenly understand why fully clothed people drowned. She grasped for the handrail. Couldn't find it. It had to be here somewhere.

Her booted feet were unsteady, unable to get grip, and the water was deeper. And all these clothes felt so constricting. Mal's instructions to appear like she was struggling suddenly wasn't so hard to do.

"Cassie?" Harrison murmured.

That's right. She'd missed her cue. "Help me!" she called.

Then a stick floated past, and she recognized those orange and brown markings, and she screamed.

Harrison pivoted sharply, losing his footing as Cassie's eyes grew large. Screaming wasn't in the script. She moved sharply, and threw a stick. Huh? That wasn't either. She cried out again, then her head ducked underwater.

No. That definitely wasn't in the script. His heart hammered. This suddenly didn't feel like acting anymore. "Cassie!" He ducked under and grasped her, boosting her to break the surface.

She sucked in air, and while Mal might call "good, good" from the sidelines, she seemed to be really panicking, gasping and choking like she'd taken in water and couldn't breathe. His role on *Beach Guard* had taught him a few skills—and the mouth-to-mouth and CPR had proved handy—and he recognized that she needed to get out of the water. Pronto.

But the creek bed was too slippery to find his footing, her skirts too heavy, so he tucked her close as the cameras rolled from all directions around them, oblivious to any danger. Her eyes were huge as she peered up at him. She was frightened, she needed him, needed him to be the strong one for a change. *Lord, help us.*

He finally got a firm footing, and lifted her, and staggered to the shore. This might've been scripted but it felt plenty real. Memories flashed of when he'd last cradled her close. This time held a similar edge of panic and concern, but without her wanting to get away from him. Instead—praise God—she snuggled in close, one hand grasping his coat, even as she hauled in deep breaths that ended in spluttering.

His heart hammered. He couldn't lose her. He'd never met anyone who could measure up to his grandma before, but this woman could. She was special, and he couldn't believe no other man had recognized that before, but he was glad for his sake that they hadn't. Because he wanted to be the one who helped her. Not just today, but every day. Cassie James might be strong, but even this tough cowgirl needed someone to support her, and he wanted to be that man. The kind of man she could trust. The kind she deserved.

Tenderness filled him as he drew her to the shore. "You're safe now." His line might be scripted, but it fitted just the same.

She snuggled closer, and he wrapped his arm around her like he was meant to, like he wanted.

But her hand was bleeding. Blood? That wasn't in the script. "Why are you bleeding?"

Her eyelids were heavy, her breathing shallow. "I saw a snake."

His heart tensed. "No way."

"Way." Her eyes closed, and her head tipped against his shoulder, and he automatically cradled her head.

Oh man. This definitely wasn't in the script. He glanced across, but Mal hadn't moved, apparently unaware of what had happened.

But there was no time to waste in for calling for a medic, especially as he knew what to do. So he laid her gently down on the grassy embankment, and ripped out his sodden handkerchief from his pocket then wrapped it tightly around her hand, pressing it in place. "I'll get help," he murmured, then grew aware of a camera in his face.

He glared at it, then glanced up, over his shoulder at where Mal stood. "She's injured!" he called.

"Yes, that's the plan."

"No, she really is," he insisted, before Cassie's other hand grasped his.

"I'll be fine," she murmured. "I'll bleed a bit but I'll be fine."

"I'll take you to the hospital."

"No, that will only cause a fuss, and it's not like this isn't similar to what we had already planned, right?"

"Cassie, no." He reached down, touched her face tenderly, his other hand holding hers tight. "No."

"Come on, Harrison, what are your lines?" Mal called.

Was he serious? Harrison stood. "That has to be a cut. Cassie just got bitten by a snake and I'm not joking. Medic!" he called.

"What?"

"Look!"

Harrison's head swiveled to where the cameraman was pointing at the creek. Sure enough, the garter snake was there again. There was a general cry and hasty exit from the vicinity, along with cries to kill it.

"Don't hurt it," he yelled. "It doesn't attack people unless threatened, and it's got an important job in the environment." Honestly, didn't these people know anything?

The medic hurried over, and soon exchanged Harrison's bandage for a real one, as Mal and the camera crew exchanged colorful views on the dangers of filming in the wild.

Mal shook his head, and moved to Cassie, regret in his features. "I'm so sorry Cassie. I never expected—oh." Heavy sigh. He turned to the medic. "Will she be okay?"

The medic helped prop her upright as her breathing slowed until she could finally suck down bottled water. She coughed again, then glanced up at Harrison, her eyes holding a plea.

"Cassie?" Harrison hunkered next to her, wrapped his arms around her shoulders. "Are you okay?"

"She will be," the medic said. "But she needs to go to hospital to make sure there's no allergic reaction."

"I'll take her."

"We need you here, Harrison," Mal said.

"No, I need to be with her."

"Harrison." Cassie's hand on his chest snagged his attention. "It's okay. I really will be fine."

This was a mistake. He should never have agreed to this. He'd only done it for his own selfish reasons, to have her with him, to have him play the hero for her damsel in distress. And look what had happened. He could never be her hero.

"Harrison?" She smiled up at him. Her good hand touched his cheek. "Thank you. My hero."

Gladness chased gratitude, as the moment filled with a heavy intensity. Suddenly he didn't care that they were surrounded by cameras and crew members or a director who was annoyed with him. He gently pushed his cheek into her hand and pressed a kiss into her palm.

Her eyes widened, and she lifted her bandaged hand to his shoulder, and he knelt beside her, drawing her up into a long embrace, her face tucked against his neck. "I'm so sorry."

"It wasn't your fault," she murmured, her lips against his jaw.

She was so forgiving, so lovely, so tender. Cassie's forthright attitude had taken some getting used to, but he wanted more of this in his life. More honesty, less pretense. And while he still wanted to continue acting, he needed someone who wasn't caught up in the fakeness of popularity or photographic perfection. He wanted—needed—a woman with zero filter, someone grounded in God and the good things of life. Someone exactly like Cassie James. Someone whose character shone from the inside out, adding an extra layer of beauty. Honest. Loyal. Everything he wanted.

Then he knew a deeper impulse to kiss her, so drew back

slightly, her lips a breath away. She smiled at him, which he took as an invitation, and closed his eyes as he gently pressed his lips to hers.

Cassie might be tough and strong, but her lips were as soft as silk, and the first silken caress soon inflamed his desire for more. "Cassie," he groaned.

"And *that's* a cut." Mal appeared above them. "Looks like that creek was a little warmer than first supposed."

Harrison smiled, remembering what had been said in the car on the way here. "I like that temperature just fine."

"Hey Mal, come look at this," the video editor called.

Harrison helped Cassie to stand. "I really want to come with you."

"I know, but if Mal wants you here—"

"Whoa. Are you serious?"

Harrison's attention shot to where Mal was frowning at the computer screen.

"Hey, you two," Mal called. "Come over here."

Harrison wrapped an arm around her shoulders. "Are you okay to walk or do you want me to carry you?"

She chuckled. "You know, I've always prided myself on being an independent woman, but I think I could get used to having a strong man carry me occasionally."

"So is that a yes?" He cocked an eyebrow.

She smirked, wrapping her arm around his waist. "Not just yet. But maybe one day."

"Cassie?" the medic called. "The car is ready."

"Look," Mal commanded.

They watched the screen where some of the raw camera footage was displayed. One of the cameras had filmed Cassie in the exact moment she'd seen the snake swim between them. There was no sound yet, but she'd gasped, screamed, then picked it up and thrown it away. It was in that moment she been bitten. Then her head ducked under the water and he had rescued her.

Mal nodded, smiling at them. "This is perfect."

Perfect that Cassie had been bitten by a snake?

"We have the double rescue, so we don't even really need to use that footage of the runaway horse before. We've got it all here. She protects you, you rescue her. Win win, wouldn't you say?"

He glanced down at Cassie, caught the way she smiled up at him, with those beautiful pink lips he wanted to explore again. He settled for pressing his lips to her forehead. "I'd say I've definitely won, that's for sure."

Sixteen

The city lights of early evening flashed in the rear view mirror as Harrison drove her home from the hospital. He held her hand, as he'd tried to ever since the incident at the creek earlier in the day. Like he wanted to touch her, to make sure she was still alive. She laughed it off, but his protectiveness was kind of lovely.

"You know I'm a big girl."

"I know. But you scared me before. I don't want to lose someone else I lo—" He coughed. "Care about."

Cassie's pulse spiked. Had he been about to say the "L" word? Oh my. He cared that much?

She peeked across. His features held a serious cast, like he would fight a thousand battles for her. "Hey." She waited until he glanced at her. "I'm not going anywhere."

He nodded, but she could tell he was still worried. Which meant they probably needed to have a few more conversations about trusting God.

She returned her gaze to look out the window. The skies were pinking to a rosy blush, streaks of gold like God had dabbled a paintbrush in gilt and was underscoring his promise with a flourish. "Isn't that sky beautiful?"

"Yeah."

Her lips lifted. "Don't you just love the big skies out here? There's so much to love about the country."

"Some things, sure." He shot her another look, mouth half curving. "I definitely love some things about the country." He winked.

Giddiness filled her, and not just because of the medication she'd taken earlier. Yep, Harrison really had that swoony thing going on.

"But not everything, I have to admit." He glanced at her. "I don't think I want to visit your creek again."

"Oh, come on. That's two snakes in twenty plus years. You can't let a little reptile stop you from having a lot of fun."

"Fun?"

She smiled, waited for him to look her way again. "Wouldn't you like to go swimming with me again?"

He exhaled heavily.

She'd take that as a "he'd think about it." And considering she didn't really want him thinking about her in a swimsuit, she should probably change the subject.

"Thanks for understanding about dinner."

"We'll save it for some day when you're feeling better."

Her hand was swollen, which meant she'd be out of action for several days. And nausea and a skin rash meant that an allergic reaction might have hit her harder than it had him. Way to go, feeling like a prize. At least it meant she wouldn't have to do any more of that acting stuff again. Once was enough, thank you.

She must've looked a sight, rocking up to the hospital with bedraggled hair and ill-fitting clothes. Mal had agreed to release Harrison to drive her, and he'd taken her to her folks first. She'd been relieved they weren't at home so they wouldn't fuss, and so she could get changed into jeans and a plaid shirt, and not go traipsing to emergency in period costume. Harrison had been thankful to exchange his sodden clothes for old ones Franklin used to wear. They might be a tad big on him, but he didn't seem to care, and his lack of vanity just reinforced how much this man had changed. Maxine had met them with Harrison's car, then they'd swapped vehicles while he drove Cassie to the hospital.

He'd been so supportive, just so wonderful, a snuggly bear whose arms she could rest in, secure, at ease. How strange that an independent woman could find joy in a strong man like this, but there it was. She did. She sighed.

"Are you feeling okay? Do I need to pull over?"

She laughed. "I'm not about to be sick in your beautiful car if that's what you're worried about."

"You can be, if you have to," he said bravely. "But I'd really rather some advance notice, all the same."

She laughed again, and his features eased. She poked his side. "What are you thinking about so seriously?"

He glanced at her, then at the road. "Do you mind if we park for a moment?"

"Um, okay."

He wasn't about to try to kiss her again, was he? Her nose wrinkled. Probably not with her awesome comment about being sick. She probably needed to work on how to do cute banter.

He pulled off the highway and down the road to the ranch, but before they got there, he steered down a little lane that led to the old Rankin place. Their place was run by a multinational corporation, and the Rankins didn't live there anymore. But she remembered the view of the stream that fed into one of the creeks of her family's ranch. She wouldn't tell Harrison which one, in case he got worried that pesky snake might find them again.

"What are you smiling about?" he asked.

"Nothing you need to worry about. But you, you wanted to tell me something, didn't you?"

He blew out a breath. Nodded. Took her hand again. "Have I ever told you much about my grandmother?"

His grandmother? "Only that she was a godly woman, and someone you miss."

He nodded, his thumb caressing the thin skin on the back of

her hand. "I do miss her. I never thought I'd meet someone as good as her." He faced her. "But then I met you."

Oh. She barely dared breathe. This sounded like one of "those" conversations.

"I know I haven't been the kind of grandson who made her proud. But I also know that I'm a new creation because of what Jesus has done, and I think she'd be glad that I now know that."

She squeezed his hand. "I'm sure she would be proud."

"And I want to make you proud. I know that my world must look so foreign to you, but I want you to know that I believe we can make this work."

"How?" she dared ask.

"I take jobs nearer here. Maybe do a Christmas movie in Vancouver with Ainsley. See you as much as I can when I'm not filming."

Maybe they could make this work, especially if he stayed nearby. Like at the western town.

"You can trust me, Cassie," he said hoarsely. "I'm not the same as who I was when I first arrived on your ranch. And I'm trusting God to lead me on."

"And He will."

He nodded. "He'll lead us both, in whatever He wants, if we listen."

"Amen," she said softly.

Silence filled the car, the sky's pink hues deepening to magenta, in one of those glorious sunsets that saw social media inundated with millions of sunset shots. But she didn't get her phone out, and neither did he. Contentment was here, the chance to breathe, and the car filled with heavenly promise. God was with them. God would guide them. And while she might have zero desire to act again, that was okay. God knew what was in her future, and knowing that, was enough for each day.

Harrison gripped Cassie's hand as her two sisters stared at her from across the living room. They'd just finished watching the Netflix adaptation of *Persuasion*, and like he'd predicted, they needed a moment to recover from the "travesty" as Poppy described it. Jess and Poppy had appeared surprised at first to see Harrison with Cassie, and he'd played it low key until the kiss at the movie's end made him forget himself and hold Cassie's hand.

Thank God her parents were understanding, as was Cassie's brother, even if Franklin had looked like he wanted to play the big brother card when they'd had dinner together a few days ago. At least they'd been supportive. Cassie's two sisters on the other hand, despite his interactions with both before, he wasn't sure of yet.

Poppy's gaze swung from Cassie to Harrison then back again. "Oh my goodness, are you serious?"

Cassie lifted up her hand that Harrison held. "Apparently so."

Jess said. "I don't know what to say."

"You don't need to say anything," Harrison said. "Except maybe congratulations."

At Cassie's quick swivel to look at him he realized his error. Congratulations? That sounded like a word reserved for big announcements. Like an engagement. Not to announce a man had found a girlfriend at last. But considering this family liked to tease, he didn't mind seeing how far he could take this.

Jess and Poppy's eyes had both rounded, like they recognized the significance of that word too. "Are you saying what I think you're saying?" Jess asked.

Harrison glanced at Cassie then kissed her hand. "That I'm the luckiest guy in the world because she said yes?"

"Cassie!" Poppy's eyes might fall from their sockets. "You've barely known the guy five minutes, and you're getting married?"

"No! Of course not."

"Maybe one day," Harrison added.

Cassie laughed and his heart jolted. That sound. He wanted

to hear that sound again. Every day. So every day he'd do what he could to bring joy to her world.

She poked him in the side. "You need to stop saying things like that and scaring my sisters."

"But it's fun to scare them."

"And you're such a good actor it's easy to believe what you say," Jess said.

"Well, this isn't acting." He turned to Cassie. "It's not acting when I say that I think you're the best woman I've ever met, and I'm so grateful that God has brought you into my life."

Sweetness creased his chest as she smiled that smile that lit up his heart. "You know, I'm almost inclined to believe you," she teased.

Uncertainty crossed his heart for a second, then he recognized her jest. "You're going to keep me on my toes, aren't you?"

"I'll do my best," she promised.

And she needed to, especially considering the industry he was in. They would have to keep submitting this relationship to God. Harrison might be a Christian, but he was a new one, and from the conversations they'd had with Ainsley and he'd had with Lincoln, he'd gathered that even Christians struggled in with all of the temptations of Hollywood. But God was faithful and Harrison would trust Him with her heart and with their future.

He dug into his pocket and pulled out his grandmother's brooch, keeping it covered.

Poppy's eyes widened again, like she actually thought he'd pulled out a ring. Well, one day he hoped to, but it sure wouldn't be in front of her sisters while the bad aroma of a dumb movie lingered like day-old popcorn in the air.

He bit back laughter as he turned to Cassie. "Remember when I was last here, and I told you I saw a photograph that reminded me of something that belonged to my grandmother?"

"I remember a lot about that day." Her voice held wryness. Then her eyes widened as if she too was wondering what he was hiding in his hand.

He didn't want her misinterpreting, so he quickly unveiled it. "It was this." He gave it to her.

"A cameo." Cassie traced the profile.

He traced her profile with his eyes. "Do you know who it reminds me of?"

"Who?"

Her breath hitched as he dared trickle a finger down her forehead, down her nose, past her lips, then ducked under her chin. She smiled.

"Oh my gosh, he's so romantic," Poppy whispered.

He smiled, his fingers cradling one of Cassie's curls that had escaped her ponytail. "You reminded me of her when I saw that picture of you all dressed up for your brother's wedding. Then again last week when you were dressed up for the show." He touched the whorl of her ear, felt her breath catch again. "So beautiful."

Cassie stared at him, her blue-green eyes wide with surprise, and what he hoped was maybe a bit of delight as well.

He arched a brow. She smiled and leaned in, and then, in front of her sisters, kissed him.

He wanted to take his fill of her, but with an audience—and with godly boundaries—knew he couldn't, so he drew back way too soon.

"Oh my gosh. Is it me or is the heat on in here?" Poppy flapped a hand in front of her face.

"It's definitely you." Jess winked at him.

He chuckled. It looked like he'd passed the sister test as well. Phew.

"Why does it seem like everyone I know is suddenly involved with all kinds of celebrities?" Poppy complained. "Franklin and Hannah, Bailey on her dance show, and now Cass and him." She pointed at Harrison.

"I'm not," Jess announced, hand in the air.

"Sure you're not. The only reason you're not is because you're too busy to open your eyes and see who's staring at you."

Jess scoffed but the pink tint to her cheeks suggested she knew exactly who Poppy was talking about.

"What is going on with Tom?" Cassie asked.

Jess shook her head. "Nothing. Just like I've said the last thousand times you've asked."

"Well, you keep us posted if that should change," Poppy said.

"You'll be the first to know, I promise."

Promise? Harrison liked the sound of that. He kissed the back of Cassie's hand again. He'd let his cowgirl keep his grandmother's cameo, and together they'd trust God's promises for their future.

The End

Want to be the first to read about Jess and her romantic adventures? Then order *A Valentine for the Vet* today.
Want to learn who steals Ainsley Beckett's heart? Then make sure you read *Faking the Shot*.
Want to discover how Franklin and Hannah got together? Then read *Fire and Ice*, book 1 in the Northwest Ice romance series.

A Note from the Author

Thank you for reading *A Cameo for a Cowgirl*, the first book in the Three Creek Ranch romance series. This is another of those 'accidental' series, where characters from *Fire and Ice* (Franklin and Hannah's story) took on a life off their own and demanded to have their stories told. So in this new series we see Franklin's three sisters negotiate love and life and how that links to their family ranch.

Three Creek Ranch with its Western Town and Back Lot is actually based on a real ranch and movie set just outside Calgary, which has been the setting of all kinds of movies and TV shows, from *Lonesome Dove* to *Shanghai Noon* to *When Calls the Heart* and *Heartland*. I had *way* too much imagining what it must be like to manage a similar ranch and movie set, and have spent many an hour checking out the CL Western Town and Backlot site. It was super fun to first introduce the ranch in *Fire and Ice* and I can't wait to see this amazing place feature again in the next book in this series, *A Valentine for a Vet*, Jessica's story.

Readers who have been keeping up to date with my books may enjoy a few references to other characters, such as Lincoln Cash (who gets his own book in *Muskoka Spotlight*, which is part of the Muskoka Romance small town series), and Sylvie, who we got to know in *The Love Penalty*. And then there's Bree and Mike who we first met in *The Breakup Project* (which coincidentally, is where Franklin first gets his cameo too), the first book in the Original Six series. Oh, and to get some more Poppy fun, make sure you check out *Pointe, Shoots, and Scores*.

To find out more about these books and behind-the-scenes inspiration, and to sign up for my newsletter, please visit my website at www.carolynmillerauthor.com

Big thanks to Jenny Glazebrook, Elisabeth Espinoza, and Carol Witzenburger for their helpful suggestions, and to May from Christian Shelves for her Canadian insights.

Reviews help other readers find new-to-them authors, so if you can spare a moment to write a quick review at Goodreads / your place of purchase, I'd be very grateful.

Make sure you check out Luc's story in the next book in the Northwest Ice romance series, *Pointe, Shoots, and Scores*.

If you enjoy Christian contemporary romance you may want to check out the books in the Original Six hockey romance series, a sweet & swoony, slightly sporty Christian contemporary romance series.

The Breakup Project
Love on Ice
Checked Impressions
Hearts and Goals
Big Apple Atonement
Muskoka Blue

Romance fans who enjoy small town life may also enjoy reading the Muskoka Romance series, that starts with *Muskoka Shores*.

I'd love for you to check out my other books and to sign up for my newsletter at www.carolynmillerauthor.com where you can be the first to learn all my book and contest news, and discover more behind-the-book details and photos. Newsletter subscribers can also get an exclusive bonus book free, so grab your copy of *Originally Yours* here.

ABOUT THE AUTHOR

Carolyn Miller lives in the beautiful Southern Highlands of New South Wales, Australia, with her husband and four children. A longtime lover of romance, especially that of Jane Austen, Georgette Heyer and LM Montgomery, Carolyn loves to write contemporary and historical romance that draws readers into fictional worlds that show the truth of God's grace in our lives.

To find out more about Carolyn's books, and to subscribe to her newsletter, please visit www.carolynmillerauthor.com

You can also connect with her at

A Cameo for a Cowgirl

A Valentine for a Vet

<u>Trinity Lakes collection</u>

Love Somebody Like You

Tangled Up in Love

Only You Can Love Me

<u>The Independence Islands series</u>

Restoring Fairhaven

Regaining Mercy

Reclaiming Hope

Rebuilding Hearts

Refining Josie

Historical:

<u>Regency Wallflowers</u>

Dusk's Darkest Shores

Midnight's Budding Morrow

Dawn's Untrodden Green

<u>Regency Brides: Legacy of Grace</u>

The Elusive Miss Ellison

The Captivating Lady Charlotte

The Dishonorable Miss DeLancey

<u>Regency Brides: Promise of Hope</u>

Winning Miss Winthrop

Miss Serena's Secret

The Making of Mrs Hale